JEAN

by

CHARLES NUETZEL

WRITING AS "FRED MACDONALD"

The Borgo Press
An Imprint of Wildside Press

MMVII

Contents

Introduction

This book has a number of things I like. It was originally titled *Illicit Beds* and had a cover by my father on it. But that has nothing to do with my liking the book. This one had to do with a Mr. Winter, who is a character in the book. His name, first of all, in a combination of my wife's maiden name, Winter, and my uncle Carl's first name, given the German version of Karl.

It is common for a writer to use people they know as characters in their stories, altered enough to never reveal their true identity, even to themselves. Generally I attempt to avoid basing my fictional folk on real-life people I know. But in this case it was too much of a temptation to capture something which was rather delightful and fitting.

A short explanation.

My uncle Carl was my father's older brother, old enough to have been my grandfather, as it turns out—and in many ways he filled that role in my childhood. He was in his eighties when he died "the ol' man of the mountains," as he had once called himself. For many years he lived in Lake Arrowhead, a mountain resort not far from Los Angeles, which now and then would even get snowed in during the winter. It's a popular place for skiers.

That is of little import concerning my using him

here. It just happens that I needed an elder man who would be both likable and able to tell a very important story that was to become a basic element of the book's theme. It is about second chances, and, even more importantly, not missing out of something important because of social pressures pushing you to do so.

So I devised this fella who told a story about his experiences as a young man in Germany. Why Germany? Because, like many others, I'm German by descent. And thus Uncle Carl was very Germanic. But more importantly, fencing has always been a sport that fascinated me. German saber fencing was at one time, and maybe even today in a limited sense, a standard challenge for some upper class males. In fact, they fought with naked blades with the idea of literally drawing blood—though not on a dangerous level. It was considered a badge of honor to have a scar on one's cheek. A rather cheeky kind of honor, has always been my somewhat doubtful thinking concerning the matter. But that's the way it was. And I used this as a part of the story that Karl Winter told a bunch of eager young listeners. He was based a lot on my memories of my uncle, a charming, intelligent story teller, very much like the one in this book.

I wanted to examine the following issues:

We all make the mistake of running from ourselves, or simply refusing to act positively on events we live through, and end up losing the most important things in our lives.

Escape had been Jean's life theme, and now she was running again, not facing reality, not facing what she was, not even knowing, for certain, if she was normal or…

> *It was ironic, Jean realized. She had gone to New York with the purpose of forgetting Al Gordon.*
> *Three years in New York had become a worse kind of hell. Loneliness was followed by a sordid, perverted affair—and now she was returning home in a desperate effort to prove that love could come to the kind of woman she had become.*

This is a story that probes deeply into the torment of a woman's mind and emotions as she attempts to escape a past she wants to forget. She runs from one sordid affair into another kind of passionate web in the arms of a man she hardly knows!

—Charles Nuetzel
Thousand Oaks, California
August 2006

JEAN, BY CHARLES NUETZEL

Chapter One

The room was lighted in soft moon glow, and there was soothing music playing from the recorder, low and sensual. The highlights, which went along the woman's semi-nude body, accented her lushly developed breasts and curvy voluptuous body.

"Man, do I need you," she moaned, standing over Frank Martin like a conqueror, a giant goddess of lust who had come out of the night to take possession of his body for the sole purpose draining it to exhaustion in sexual combat.

She raised her arms, so that the thrust of her large breasts surged upwards, invitingly.

"We're good together, the two of us!" she half sighed. "You're the best man I've known!"

Frank felt a tingling at the lustful offering of this woman's body.

Kay Clifford isn't a gentle lover, Frank mused as he watched her hands slide lingeringly along her silken body.

"You're quite a woman!" Frank laughed huskily, automatically reaching out for her.

She glided back, saying: "Not so fast! I want to tease you a little."

Taking that body was exciting; but nothing much beyond that.

After the long build-up of dinner and cocktails at the *Beachcomber*, then the dancing at the *Huntington Hotel* and the final exodus to his apartment, Frank didn't want to play games. He had been with Kay too many and felt like the drunk who takes more drinks because he doesn't know better. Physically he was excited by Kay, but bored with the routine. She enjoyed teasing a man; to her that was some kind of erotic thrill; and at first it had been interesting. Now it was just a routine without much personal impact.

Kay's fingers tucked under the top of her panties. "Wanna see?"

Frank waved his hand, inviting her to come closer.

"No, love! You have to wait a little!" She started peeling down the panties. "Just watch!"

Finally Kay slipped the panties down over her wide hips, then along full thighs. She stepped out of them, and threw the lacy cloth away. It disappeared from sight into the blackness of the room that surrounded her highlighted form.

Her eyes continued to stare teasingly into his as she once more cupped her hands under those large breasts. "They want you, too, love!"

Finally, Kay's bra slipped off and then disappeared from sight into the blackness of the room, which surrounded her highlighted form.

He couldn't really see her lips smiling sensually, or the point of her tongue moistening their surface to a soft glistening shine, or see the raw flame of desire sparkling in the hidden depths of her dark green eyes, as if a furnace were burning brightly beyond their surface. He didn't have to see all that to know it was what took place in the few seconds in which Kay stood unmoving, her head bent down in his direction. As hot as Kay was, Frank found their relationship slightly tiresome. He wanted something more than mere sex with a woman. And that, in reality was all she was: a sexy body.

Instead of mentally picturing her standing there in the dimness of the room, his mind played strange tricks with him. For a moment he saw another lovely woman standing there, like some phantom. It was illusion, but delightful. A thrill shot through him at the mental image. This was a woman he could really get interested in. It was an image that had been teasing him a lot these last days. Ever since Joe Hanson had shown him her photo a week before.

A girl who had golden hair and dark, almost hauntingly lovely, frightened eyes. An oval face with high cheekbones, a mouth that was just a little too full to be perfect, but still lovely.

Jean MacManners. She'd been captured in his brain, like a fiery, lovely, welcoming brand. He hadn't even met her. Yet. Tomorrow was the magic day! That's when he would meet this charmingly, haunting woman and discover just what it really was that had captured his imagination so vividly. Fantasy was one thing; reality another.

But why should her image be pestering him in the middle of a real-life seduction with Kay?

"Frank oh, Frank," Kay's low, rich voice cut into his thoughts. She was leaning down near him, her breasts swaying within inches of his lips.

He leaned forward, smothering his lips against her flesh. "Oh, Frankie, you're *good.*" she mur-

11

mured breathlessly, "So good."

She drew him to her, and in the next minutes they were locked together in a continual series of caresses and kisses.

Yet his mind simply kept drifting away from what they were doing, as if a part of him were totally bored.

He continued to see imagines of Jean teasing his mind, even as his body was reacting, intensely responding to Kay's love-making. Her hands, lips and body captured him in a series of loving caresses, mad, passion hungry kisses. Then finally she lifted, moaning, and she totally envelop him. It felt as if she had swallowed him whole. For a few deliciously wild moments they shared the fury of mutual ecstasy.

Then it was finished, spent out.

Neither of them moved for a long time, only sliding apart after that one last instant of pleasure had rippled through them. It was a long while before Frank's mind began to organize thoughts out of the gray mass of nothingness that had been the aftermath of love-play. And again his mind pictured the young blonde with the large dark eyes whom he would be meeting the next day.

God, he could hardly wait!

"You're a lucky brute," Joe Hanson had told him with envy. "She's a real great woman!"

"But does she like to be—well, nicely put: enjoyed?" Frank had wanted to know.

Joe Hanson told him: "She ran away from an affair here when she went to New York!"

There was some doubt in Frank's mind whether Jean MacManners was going to be an easy conquest, but the years of experience he had chalked up during his youth didn't leave any doubt in his mind that there wasn't a girl in the world that he couldn't have one way or another. And from what he had seen of Jean, from her picture, she would be well worth a lot of effort.

"Oh, love—" Kay mannered softly into his ear. "You love me?"

Frank felt himself go tense and cold inside. "Now, baby, don't get *that* way."

Kay sat up, gripping his arm: "Why not?"

"I've gone over that with you. I'm not the marrying kind."

"Oh, you're maddening!" she exclaimed heatedly.

"You aren't the marrying kind, either. You're just fooling yourself!"

"And why not?" she demanded tartly.

"Because there's not a man who could keep up with you," he explained.

"Oh, you rat!" she sighed, clawing at his back with intense savageness. Her nails cut into the flesh.

"You drive a girl wild," she choked in a rasp. "A girl could really go for you. Frank. You know that? A girl would be lucky to have a man like you!" Her voice was light and joking, but serious nonetheless.

"There've been women before who tried to hook me," he warned softly.

"Bet there hasn't been any like me!"

"Not many," he offered.

"That's not a nice thing to say, Frank! It was mean!" she pouted. "You're supposed to tell me I'm the best. Something real nice, like that. Like I'm special…"

"Every woman has something special to offer. Every woman has something to make her different. It has nothing to do with *better*. Better in what way?"

"You're a bastard. You know I'm crazy about you." Her voice was so throaty and husky that he almost laughed; it was too affected to have the conviction of truth. But that was Kay. Then she was all over him again, demandingly charging his own body to take her on, full blast. If nothing else, she was one hell of a wild woman. And it continued until both of them fell exhaustedly unconscious in one another's arms.

The morning sun was the next thing that Frank was aware of. He stirred in bed and then felt the other form next to his. For a moment he couldn't remember who it was.

"It's eight-thirty!" she exclaimed in a tired voice.

Frank moved from the bed. "We still have a little over half an hour to get to the office; we can catch something for breakfast during the coffee break."

Kay looked at him as she slowly stood.

"That was really something," she announced, happily patting his thigh. "You sure are a hard one!"

Frank simply nodded as he started getting dressed. His mind had already lost interest in Kay.

"You doing anything tonight?" she inquired boldly.

"Sorry. A party at the Hanson's," he told her in an almost irritated tone.

"You don't have to snap my head off!" Kay

14

countered, obviously hurt and angry.

"I'm sorry, I was just thinking."

There was a long silence as they got dressed. When Frank was starting out of the bedroom, Kay stopped him, with:

"Can't you call it off—tonight?" Her eyes were intimate promises. "Or—or make it a short visit? I'll—wait."

Frank slowly shook his head. "I'm sorry."

But he wasn't. One evening every three or four days was about all he could take of Kay.

"Oh, damn! I could go on like that for days— without end!" Then Kay shrugged her shoulders, the action bobbing her breasts slightly. "Well, there'll be other times. Maybe some weekend—in the mountains or at the beach—or just at a motel or hotel or yours or my place."

"Maybe," he agreed absently.

Fifteen minutes later they were in his car driving down the Hollywood Freeway to *Davis, Martin & Gordon, Insurance.*

Chapter Two

The blonde woman in the high fashion black dress, sitting in the seat next to the window, looking thoughtfully out at the expanse of the world slipping under the large six-jet liner, seemed from all outwards appearances quite calm and relaxed. There was no surface indication of the inner torment that was churning through her guilt-laden mind. She was just a wonderfully voluptuous woman with the look of high fashion, sitting, half asleep, waiting for the long flight from New York to finally come to an end and bring her to Los Angeles International Airport. But her mind was tormented, lost in deep thought.

It's ironic, Jean MacManners realized. She'd gone to New York with the purpose of forgetting Al Gordon, the man she had made the foolish mistake of loving.

The shock of learning he was married and not planning on ever getting a divorce had been too much! She'd frantically run from Los Angeles, getting as far away from the man who had turned her on not only emotionally, but sexually. She'd sworn never to give herself to a man in that way as long as she lived.

To this day she'd managed to keep this promise; though hadn't turned off the sexual fires of her body.

Shame and disgust knifed through Jean.

I've run before and now I'm running again! She cursed herself, bitterly.

She'd learned a lot since first being seduced by Al Gordon and his slick line, his body beautiful.

Nervously, Jean lighted a cigarette, tried to clear her thoughts of Al Gordon. He had all but ruined her life, and now—far more terrible—she was running from the perverted pathway he'd forced her down.

She had known very little about sex before meeting Al, and she learned in New York that there were other ways to gain emotional and sexual satisfaction that didn't require a man.

The bitterness she'd experienced at having been used like a cheap foolish whore had set her up for Debra.

She took a deep drag on the cigarette, looked out the window. But her eyes were not focusing on the fleecy whiteness of the clouds, but rather on the mental image of the round-faced redhead who had drawn her into the perverse world of the Lesbian and the strange sensual pleasure that it had to offer.

Oh, Debra, you were wonderful! she thought despondently, not even wanting to admit this to herself. Yet it was impossible to ignore. A fact was a fact.

Debra had been overwhelmingly passionate last night, she remembered. It was their goodbye party and their final connection.

They had drunk cocktails before and after dinner. By ten they walked into the bedroom they had shared together for months, undressed and found each other in the semi-darkness. The intimate nearness of their bodies, as they slipped under the covers for the last time, had filled Jean MacManners with a mixture of chaotic emotions.

Then Debra's delicate hands were moving over her body with a gentle caressing, a loving care, building the longing and the needing into intense hunger. Later they had cried and clung to one another. She had continued to sob until the unhappy knot in her throat had momentarily melted away.

"Can't you please stay?" Debra had begged in her low, feminine voice, hanging longingly to Jean.

"I can't, Debbie, you know that. You know why. This isn't the kind of life for me. I can't have those things I wanted so desperately out of life."

Anger and fear flared in Debra's large blue eyes. "Why? Why are you doing this to me?" Then the expression on her face softened and she relaxed. "I understand. But just don't forget—there are ways to have a baby, if you really want to. I don't know what I'm going to do without you!"

There were ways of getting pregnant, or even adopting a child. But she believed children needed a father and a mother; they needed a lot of love and a lot of affection and a lot of help and understanding and attention as they grew up. And there was another fact that her mind kept pointing out to her: before meeting Debra she had *liked* men. Debra had never experienced pleasure with a man and knew nothing else but Lesbian love. Luckily for Jean, Debra was the kind of woman that could love very deeply and unselfishly, wishing only happiness for the loved one; otherwise it might not have been as easy for Jean to decide to return to Los Angeles and attempt to recapture the life she had lived before going to New York. In time she was sure to meet somebody.

Just not like the man she'd left L.A. to escape.

Al had used her. She had merely been a plaything to him, nothing to take seriously. A lark. All her life she had believed that sex should be only experienced with somebody you love, somebody that you felt was special. Al had taught her differently, in the end. And Debra had expanded on the reality that a person could find a great amount of emotional satisfaction with another person, even of the same sex. But, in the long run, it simply wasn't enough.

Now things seemed so changed. The three years in New York had been a worse hell than the one from which Jean had tried to escape in Los Angeles. The secretary job at *Davis, Davis & Sons* had brought her enough money for a small apartment and food; just barely enough to survive. At first, Jean went out with a couple of men, at first just to enjoy a free meal. But when they made passes she had frozen up, making it clear that she "wasn't that kind of girl."

Which, in truth, wasn't quite a lie.

Jean had been determined to keep away from any affairs, any involvements that might hurt her.

Then she had met Debra Channings, another secretary working for *Davis, Davis & Sons*. At first they had just been good friends and then one evening when Jean was at Debra's apartment the other girl managed to pull off the slickest seduction that Jean had ever experienced.

First drinks and then accidental physical contacts and then more drinks. Finally more caressingly "accidental" touches. And the sudden strange awareness that physical contact with Debra was rather nice. Before the evening was half over they were in Debra's bedroom, lying naked on the bed. The drinks had made Jean far too high to really care about anything, let alone what was happening. This was something new and *exciting* because of its newness. And safe. She was aware of being intimately caressed, but not feeling guilt that it was a woman doing the caressing. For months she hadn't experienced any sexual relations and the mere physical need had been strong enough to overwhelm her slack resistance. Debra's love-making was amazingly skilled, gentle, caring, slowly approached with simple kisses on the cheek, to a more sensual kiss on the mouth that was followed a slow exploration over her whole body.

Unlike a man, Debra had continued loving her in an amazingly skilled way, slowly building the fires to such a wild peak that she was clawing at the bed in her agonized pleasure. Debra's arms had embraced her thighs, delicate caressing hands placed low on her stomach.

Later, Debra had shown her a dildo, which was very large and long.

Jean had been shocked, but strangely excited by the sight of that fake organ. "It looks so real!"

"That's what is so great about it! It can be terribly good when used by a real artist! Most girls think I'm just great!"

And she was. Amazingly skilled. A true artist of love.

Jean had responded to the erotic stimulation of the dildo.

It was a wonderful experience having that dildo

moving so expertly in her. Al had never been able to last so long. It had been heavenly. Especially after the long tortured months without any sexual outlet of any kind other than self-masturbation. And, she had suddenly discovered, and willing admitted, Lesbian love was far better than masturbation.

It was a wonderful experience that evening. Later she felt the guilt, yet managed to hold it back for a long time; it would be forced downwards until it had no effect over her life, and then would return, each time with greater force, each time almost overwhelming her. Debra had convinced her to not give up, to try to make it work, so they could have one another.

And Jean had tried so very hard, but finally it wasn't possible to contain the guilt any longer. She would find herself wandering the streets after work, dreading the night with Debra.

Angrily, Jean forced her mind to the present. What she was leaving in New York had to stay there, where it belonged, in her past.

Isolated.

Dead.

Sleep clouded over Jean's mind, giving her momentary rest, and the long flight to Los Angeles was almost over before she stirred. Her dark, large eyes looked down nervously at the tiny gold wristwatch on her arm which Debra had given her last Christmas. It had been an expensive gift, but not improperly so, considering their relationship.

It was eight-twenty-five, a little less than twenty minutes before she would be stepping out of the plane and meeting her older sister, Mary Hanson; thirty minutes or so later she would be unpacking her clothing in the small extra room which had been offered and promised her as a haven from the last three years.

"Will you fasten your safety belt, miss," the voice of the stewardess interrupted her thoughts.

Jean turned her eyes away from the window and looked at the woman in the gray-blue uniform who was leaning over her. The smiling expression on the stewardess' face chilled Jean.

She knows! She's one of us—and making a pass—a subtle suggestion with her eyes!

Jean tensed inwardly. Then she laughed, nervously.

"Something wrong, miss?"

"No no. Thank you!" Jean said, a little too loud. Her imagination was overworking; her guilt was causing her to fancy the impossible. There was no way for the stewardess to know about her. A Lesbian didn't have a neon sign flashing on and off in front of her, announcing what she was. It was impossible to tell a normal girl from a Lesbian. The women who looked mannish and were a little forceful, with low voices, and dressed in slacks all the time, were usually the hottest bed companions for men—while the girl who was slim, delicate and very feminine, like Debra, could turn out to be the most dedicated Lesbians. The sexy woman with large thrusting breasts and a voluptuous body, like herself, could be all woman, possessing the normal passions which were a woman's right to feel, or could be the most mannish Lesbian lover.

In her case, what was the real truth?

Which one are you, Jean MacManners? she inquired inwardly as the plane started to circle down-

22

wards over Los Angeles International Airport.

Jean watched the blue Pacific swing into view through the window, stretching far below them out to the horizon. In moments the plane had raced away from the ocean and then circled down to the landing strip and was settling onto the ground.

There was a screech of tires and the slight jarring sensation. Then the plane taxied along the runway and glided toward the end of the landing field.

Jean felt the need for a cigarette—or a drink. The prospect of meeting her sister and the woman's new husband didn't hold much excitement for her. But this was her last chance to face reality and discover what she really was, strait woman or Lesbian.

It was several minutes before the jet came to a stop and the stewardess instructed the passengers that they could leave.

Jean slowly unstrapped herself and reluctantly stood. As she stepped out of the plane, and then down the ramp to the ground, she felt a sense of gnawing doubt. The feeling grew as she spotted the dark hair of her sister in the small crowd that had gathered at the gate. Then it was replaced by a terrible sense of being alone, helpless and lost.

Will the answer really be here? Jean wondered anxiously as she stepped through Gate 8 and moved toward the tallish woman with whom she had grown to maturity, who she knew was the only person— outside of Debra—who cared anything about her— but also, like Debra, could hardly really help.

* * * * * * *

The drive to the Hanson home was a mixture of

long awkward silences and sputtering conversation. It was a little over half an hour drive from the airport, and Jean had a long time to become aware of the stilted atmosphere between her sister and her new husband. The conversational lags were tense with heavy energy, tight with the undercurrent of silent, seething emotion. Nothing was said about how happy and excited they were to see Jean. It seemed as if they would much rather she had stayed in New York. Mary kept asking questions about New York and life there; she didn't know about Debra, and Jean had no plans of saying anything about it. This was her own private battle, her own disturbing secret.

Finally they arrived at their destination and Jean was shown to the room she would be using during her stay at the Hanson household.

Jean's older sister closed the door behind them and then leaned exhaustedly against it.

Neither woman said anything for a long time, but there was the tense, silent knowledge that something was terribly wrong. Mary let out a deep tired sigh, which flattened her already delicately shaped chest.

"Oh, I'm truly glad to see you," Mary cried, stepping forward and folding her arms around Jean.

Jean felt a sense of nervousness in having been suddenly cast in the role of comforter, when she needed help and understanding herself. But Jean's arms circled her sister and there was a terrible sense of guilt, because the woman's body had a surprisingly sensual quality about it. Not because it was Mary, her sister, but because it was a female form clutching to hers. Instinct tore at Jean to push Mary

24

away, but she fought down this anguished impulse.

"Something wrong?" she heard her own voice questioning. "Want to talk about it?"

"I don't know...I just don't know." Mary fell silent for a few minutes and then after taking a handkerchief from her dress pocket and drying her eyes she said, "Please forgive me I know you have problems of your own."

"Sometimes it's better to get it off your chest, Mary," Jean told her, inwardly fighting off the aching need to scream.

"Maybe."

That one word had a hopelessness to it which shocked Jean out of her own feelings of self-pity, jarring her to the realization that possibly her sister had issues as shattering emotionally as Jean felt her own to be.

"Is it about you and Joe?" she inquired gently.

Mary nodded and then the words gushed out in a sudden torrent. "I know it's all my fault."

"Nothing is *all* anybody's fault—there are two—"

"No! No. It's my fault. But...I can't help what I am. Can I?" She paused long enough to give the question force and then quickly continued. "You can't blame a man for wanting a normal married life—and if I—if I find that I can't please him in *that* way...oh, I've tried. How I've tried. Everything! I even went to a doctor and he gave me shots and things but I just can't help it. And I do love him so much!"

It was like suddenly being slapped and slapped over and over again. Jean felt a dizzy nausea, a terrible inner anguish. There wasn't any question about what her sister was trying to tell her. Mary hadn't come out and said, *"I'm frigid, and afraid Joe is stepping out on me,"* but that was what she meant.

"What can I do?" Mary cried in a small voice that was so filled with desperation that Jean forgot her own problems.

"I don't know what to tell you, Mary. Maybe if I knew the answer to that I wouldn't be here now. People have to face themselves honestly and try to be *themselves,* not what they think they should be or others think they should be—but who knows their real self?"

Mary shook her head and then half smiled. "Tragedy is over! This isn't the time to be crying on each other's shoulders. Just forget what I said. How'd you like a drink?"

"Sis, you just hit the spot! That is one thing my mouth was watering for all during the flight from New York!"

"Oh, by the way," Mary said, pausing at the door, "we're having a party tomorrow night. I hope you don't mind, but I invited a young man over for you. Frank Martin. He's a *dream* and very popular. He's seen your photo and—well, he was more than interested in meeting you."

Panic raced through Jean, but she managed to nod and smile.

"That's all right," she told her sister in a controlled voice. Then she thought, as the door closed, *maybe it's best, because I'll have to start someplace. Maybe this Frank Martin will turn out to be the answer to my problems. At least he could be a start!*

It was almost exciting, wondering what it might

be like with a man; just for kicks, like she'd allowed herself to be with Debra: but with a difference. This time it would be a normal, sexual thing between a man and woman.

She wondered if any man could be as good to her as the Debra and her dildo.

Of course, she thought with total surprise, *it had to be better. A dildo didn't have an orgasm!*

For the first time since leaving Los Angeles for New York, she realized that such thoughts had never really entered her mind. Not until now. What did it feel like having a man? She had almost forgotten. In fact, she couldn't really even remember that far back. Not the details, anyway.

She shook off the thoughts and decided to wait and find out what happened between her and Frank Martin. He might not even like her. Or she might not even like him. Chance were it would be a dud or, perhaps, just an awkward evening. Actually it wasn't a date, merely a party with an equal number of males and females.

Then a small knowing smile formed on her lips. Any man would like a piece of her action—or any attractive woman's body—if it was made obvious as hell she wanted him. Men were basic. Not as complex as a woman. All she'd have to do was turn herself on full blast. And a male would be dumbly helpless to her charms.

Suddenly she felt a swift sense of power, realizing how much actual power a woman did have over a man. Short of rape, a woman couldn't be seduced without first offering it up to her possible partner. All she had to do was keep her legs crossed and the man could simply squirm in his pity pot of hot desire.

A laugh almost burst out from her lips; but she choked it down.

Then reconsidering the whole thing felt a bit silly and guilty.

Then a nagging doubt caught in her throat: *Would she find it possible to give herself even in a physical way to* any *man?*

Chapter Three

For a moment Jean couldn't remember where she was. Sleep was still numbing and confusing her thoughts. She lay there in the strange bed, trying hard to place her surroundings.

A dry taste was in her mouth and a throbbing ache pounding at her temples.

You drank too much last night, she thought.

For a moment longer her memory was blank.

There was only the throbbing hangover, which was all too familiar to her. Then as memory returned, she felt a sense of emptiness, which cried out for the delicate feminine form of Debra Channings. But it wasn't there.

Slowly, the fog of sleep drifted away and Jean sat up in bed. She looked around the room. Concern replaced that other emotion which had been in her mind—concern about Joe Hanson, her new brother-in-law. There wasn't any doubt in Jean's mind that if given the opportunity Joe might willingly step right into an intimate relationship with her. Panic rushed in and for a moment she felt a sudden mental haziness.

What kind of new trap had she gotten into by coming to Los Angeles?

All yesterday afternoon and evening, Joe, a huge

29

brute of a man with dark thick hair and a stupid
animal look about his face, had been following
every move she made, stripping her body bare with
his dark brooding eyes. He was a sexy hunk of
male-animal! No doubt about that. It seemed as if
electricity were waving between them—an intimate
electric charge that had no business being there.

He hadn't said anything, or shown by action,
any indication as to what he was thinking or desir-
ing, but the evidence was all too obviously printed
on his face every time his eyes swept along her figure. He wasn't the kind of man that Jean would have
picked for her sister to marry. Joe wasn't dumb; one
realized that in talking with him. He could cover
any subject that came up in a conversation with the
air of a man who has read a lot and easily remembered what he read. Jean hadn't found out what he
did for a living. In letters, Mary had said he was in
the transportation business, but Jean felt it went further than that for he didn't have the mind of a truck
driver, or the slack attitude of a workingman. Visu-
ally, he appeared a below average truck driver, unable to handle anything intellectually deeper than a
comic book, but his mind was sharp and fast.

Shaking herself, Jean slowly slipped from the
bed and walked to the small half-bath off the bedroom. She undressed, and then, after turning on the
water in the shower and waiting for it to warm,
stepped into the stall and let the prickly spray work
over her body. It was caressing heat, teasing the
nerve endings, playing games with her muscles as
they moved smoothly under the delightful pleasure
it gave.

Twice she had been in a shower with Debra,

once with Al. In each case the experience had been quite thrilling.

With Debra it was a soft surging of two female bodies wetly clinging.

With Al, she had thrilled to the dampness of his hard body.

Jean attempted to mentally remember the feel of a man inside her. It was difficult!

Jean's hands were caressing between her legs. A thrill waved through her.

She tried to stop her hands, but they continued caressing. Mentally she imagined Debra touching her, then quickly tried to visualize a man. And instantly the picture to her brother-in-law formed.

Horrified, Jean sank back against the wall of the shower stall, sick inside.

She felt cheap and disgusted with herself. It wasn't so much the masturbating but the mental images that flinted across her mind while doing so.

Joe Hanson was the kind of man who could fire almost any woman with a natural animal desire.

She wondered about her sister. How could a normal female ever be frigid towards Joe Hanson?

It would be so easy to seduce her sister's husband; all too easy. But she hadn't dropped that far; not yet. And prayed to God she never would!

Still, the hot wanting and needing for normal sexual release was building to wild emotional and physical pain within her whole being. It was already beginning to envelop all her thoughts.

Why should she be so focused on such things? She wasn't some oversexed nympho.

The fact was, running from the affair with Debra had left a terrible hole in her mind, life, and her emotional needs. And that was also a sexually charged deep well.

Only a little over twenty-four hours, and she was "wanting" someone in such a desperate way that her mind grabbed at any wild image. A fantasy lover. A make-believe male animal that just happened to look exactly like her brother-in-law; who just happened to be in the same house. But it was pure fantasy; and her own phantom mental image that was, no doubt, nothing like reality.

Somebody had told her it was okay to hold fantasies, as long as it never went beyond that. But this was different.

She needed to get her head on straight.

She knew her interest in Joe was an artificial need, brought on by the pressure of being in new and confusing surroundings and frantic to prove to herself that she was a woman responsive to a man's body. That was normal enough.

She simply needed some other male image to feed her fantasies.

And what made it even more difficult was the fact she had so little to do. She was used to working: spending her daily hours in an office—endlessly socializing. It wouldn't be possible to continue staying here at her sister's home for very long. She'd go quietly crazy.

The caressing water brought her mind back to actual need. She felt suddenly so very alone, helpless and insecure.

Oh, Debra, her mind cried. *How I wish you were here!*

Then she hurriedly rejected the desire.

No! I have to see this thing out by myself!

Finally, Jean took the bar of soap and began to work over her body, cleaning it. The touch of her fingers reminded her of Debra. The feel of her breasts and body reminded her of Debra's breasts and body.

In desperation, Jean threw the soap onto the floor, turned off the water and stepped from the shower stall. In moments she dried herself, dressed and went out to the living room, where Mary was sitting watching television.

* * * * * * *

The afternoon was long and intermittently given to conversation between the two sisters as they prepared things for the evening meal and party that would follow. Yet there was an awkwardness about it that bothered Jean and she was glad when Joe came home.

It seemed as if Mary was too happy to see her husband, and Jean could almost read the relief in her eyes that said: *Thank God! Now the responsibility of keeping a conversation going isn't mine any more.*

Joe had brought several bottles of whiskey and soda water to add to the refreshments which Jean had helped her sister make for the party that was to begin at nine.

Dinner was stilted, but the edgy thickness of the atmosphere slowly began lifting after they had consumed a round of highballs. Jean went to her room to change into a cocktail dress, and as she was putting it on she heard lightly heated conversation taking place in the living room between Mary and Joe. She couldn't make out what it was they were talking about, but from the soft tone and the tense quality of their voices she couldn't help thinking it was about her. As much as she hated to admit it, her stay at the Hanson house couldn't be a prolonged visit. There was already too much tension and conflict taking place in her sister's home.

Sighing, Jean went to the small half-bath and looked into the mirror over the sink. In the next fifteen minutes she remade her face and was just beginning to step into the living room when the front doorbell buzzed like a little hissing snake.

"That should be Frank—I asked him to conic early." Joe exclaimed, rushing from the hallway behind Jean. He moved to the front door and opened it.

A tall, redheaded man, with angular, cleanly cut features, stepped into the house. In the first fleeting impression, Jean felt a little nervousness and irritation about the assured way the man moved toward her.

"You must be Jean MacManners," the man announced brightly. "You're even more beautiful than your picture!"

"And you're Mr. Martin?" Jean inquired in a stiffly formal voice, looking evenly into the man's light blue eyes. For a moment the two of them gazed at each other without saying anything.

Joe joined them. "Well, I see you two already know each other." He paused for only one beat and then asked, "How about a drink?"

Frank Martin nodded and Joe waited until Jean admitted that she would like one too, then he left them by themselves.

"You can call me Frank," the redheaded giant

announced in a friendly and warm voice.

Jean had the impulse to tell him she believed people who have just met should not call each other by their first names, but realized that it would offend his ego to the point of ruining the whole evening not only for him and herself, but for Mary and Joe. He was their friend and she didn't have the right to be openly nasty to him. Instead of saying anything at all, she merely nodded and smiled shallowly.

"I've heard a lot about you, Jean—you don't mind if I call you Jean, do you?" He didn't pause long enough for her to object. "Anyway, I feel I know you—and I guess you don't know a thing about me."

She merely shrugged that off and tried to look mildly interested.

There was a stilted silence and then Frank shuffled nervously and his face became serious. "Okay, I'm clowning! I'm sorry. Just that I always have the uneasy feeling people are talking about me behind my back."

"Don't you think people are concerned about their own problems, rather than thinking and talking about *you?*" There was a biting edge to Jean's voice.

"No! I didn't mean it's complimentary. A man like me gets some pretty nasty remarks made about him. I meant, sometimes women get the wrong idea. That's what I'm really trying to explain. They're told the only thing I'm interested in is…well…to put it politely—getting them into a compromising position. That's not so!"

"Isn't it?" Jean asked, raising one eyebrow.

"It is!" Joe exclaimed, laughingly stepping up with two highballs. "He's a rake! Just watch out for him, Jean. He has a reputation with the women that terrifies all! Except those anxious to be...well, to have a man for other purposes than marriage."

"See what I mean?" Frank pointed out, his voice resigned.

For the first time, Jean saw something behind the surface mask and shell of cocksureness that was so crudely marked on Frank's face. His eyes were half veiled, trying to hide the reaction to Joe's words. A flicker of resentment seemed hidden there under the surface.

After that a long conversation was exchanged between Joe and Frank. During the next half hour Jean learned something about both men. Joe owned his own trucking company and Frank Martin was a partner in an insurance firm. His company insured Joe's trucks and it was through this relationship that they had gotten to know each other. Before Mary had married him, Joe had run around with Frank; they had been pretty close buddies. As they were talking, Frank kept glancing over to Jean, running his eyes along her figure, which was well displayed in a blue dress. Once Frank broke away from the conversation long enough to say to her: "You're quite a beautiful woman."

She couldn't help being pleased.

As much as Jean hated to admit it, Frank had an air about him, besides his outstandingly good looks, that attracted her in a vaguely exciting way. His body was big, but leanly built. She could only guess that every muscle was steel hard, but she was pretty sure of it.

36

When Mary finally stepped into the living room the conversation was turned away from "man talk" to social subjects in which the girls could enter. As if cued by the conversational change, the doorbell rang. Mary answered it. A couple, introduced as the Browns, came into the living room. Drinks were offered and accepted by all and the party atmosphere finally developed. It wasn't until the third and last couple had arrived, though, that Frank Martin managed to trap Jean in the kitchen. She had gone for another drink.

"Don't think I haven't noticed," he greeted.

Startled, Jean asked, "What?"

"You," he grinned.

"So, what does that mean?" Jean inquired nervously.

"Well, we got off to a bad start. I didn't think it good to push until things began swinging. Know what 1 mean?"

Jean turned and looked at Frank, painfully aware of the fact that this was a man many women paid a lot of attention to: the type that they chased. A beautiful stud. She was also sure that he would take any woman into a bedroom and give her his full personal attention, and then forget about her a few hours later. Strangely, the idea was intriguing, considering her own personal confusion about what she was or wasn't, what she wanted out of life. It was the ease with which such an intimate relationship could be entered into, and forgotten, without strings, that tempted her mind to consider making it easy for him.

"You have any plans?" Frank inquired, putting ice in his now empty glass.

"About what?"

"About the next weeks?" He let the question hang as he poured whiskey into his glass and added soda.

She didn't answer.

"What I mean to say," he continued, turning his eyes and full attention to Jean. "is that if you are interested in seeing the town consider me as a possible escort. I'd just love that kind of assignment."

For a moment Jean felt like laughing. But what troubled her was that she didn't know what was really so funny.

"I've seen Los Angeles. I was born and raised here."

"Oh, yes, that's right. Foolish of me to forget." He laughed uneasily and then added, "In any case, maybe you'd find it interesting to see what's been changed since you left town."

She shrugged. The idea of having a date with a man, possibly getting into an intimate relationship with him, neither excited nor startled her. The fact was, she didn't know what she wanted. He might be as good as any man!

"What do you do besides see how many women you can have?" she inquired blandly.

Frank's eyes narrowed with surprise, then he smiled. "Is there anything else *necessary?*"

"It's not the only thing in the world!" she pointed out.

For a moment he stared seriously at her. "Okay, so I've been a little flippant. Tell you what. If you can put up with me for a whole evening by ourselves, I'll show you some of the things I'm most interested in, outside of women."

38

"You asking me out for a date?" she inquired mockingly.

"Okay, if that's the way you want it. How about next Friday evening?"

"I don't know…what did you have in mind?"

"Well, if that's not taking the rocket out of the ship!" he exploded. "You have to be bribed! Kinda like a woman saying, when invited for dinner at your home: what are you serving, before answering. Want to know before accepting." He hesitated, frowning, and then slowly added, "I think you're the kind of woman who likes surprises."

Jean suddenly relaxed and laughed. "Okay that's a date! What time?"

"Oh, about seven-thirty."

"Before or after dinner?"

"Before, naturally. You don't think I'd ask a woman out for an evening without the idea of feeding her, do you?"

They talked for a while longer and then a couple of the other guests stepped into the kitchen and conversation started among the four of them.

During the rest of the evening the events took the normal course of most parties, bringing the conversation through the wide subjects of world affairs, sports, politics, and then finally to the most intriguing of party subjects, sex.

The drinking had been pretty heavy by the time sex arrived into the conversation. Everybody was now sitting in the living room. The lights had been dimmed and music was playing softly from the radio.

"I think there is a lot to be said about sex!" Mr. Brown exclaimed when the subject was just lightly brought up.

A snickering filled the room. But Brown waved his hand; he was quite serious. "There are a lot of byways to the sexual side of life. Now you take a group of people like us here tonight," he continued. "Four married couples and two singles! Now, each of us has a different idea about sex and things..." He thought for a moment and then, having chosen his words with apparent care, continued, "Well each of us has a different set of beliefs of right and wrong. Each of us works on what we believe to be right and wrong. Each of us thinks that we are right about what we believe, and all the others *wrong!*"

Frank broke in with, "That's not necessarily so. Everybody can have a different set of morals, but doesn't have to believe that all other points of view are wrong. It all depends on where you stand—first, from the division of married and single people. If you are married happily or unhappily. If you are single happy or unhappy. That gives you four slices of truth. Each slice will have a different set of values and a different set of desires.

"Now take the man who isn't married. Either he has affairs or he doesn't. Either he wants to get married or he doesn't. If he likes sex and doesn't particularly want to get married—he either has affairs with only the girls he might want to marry—or only with the girls he doesn't want to marry. Being a single man he must consider if he thinks that a woman should be a virgin before marriage or not—and that will decide his actions!"

Mrs. Carter, a matronly appearing woman of thirty-two, who had the look of being a little stiff, broke into the conversation. "I can't help thinking that a woman *should* have the same rights as a man! I don't like the double standard!"

There was a silence after her statement and then suddenly Mr. Brown ran his hand through his thin hair and turned toward Jean. "What do you think about that? Do you believe in the double standard—or not?" When she didn't answer right away, he added, "I asked you because you're single."

Mary quickly interposed, "That puts Jean on a terrible—"

"I'm sorry," Mr. Brown backed down. "I didn't mean—"

Jean raised her hand, said, "That's all right. I can answer it *without* personally committing myself."

She was thoughtful for an instant and then carefully chose her words. "I'll put it this way: what goes on between two people in private is nobody's business but the two involved—as long as they aren't hurting anybody but themselves—whether they are married or not—and as long as each is fully consenting to their activities."

There was an awkward silence for a moment and then Joe took up the ball. "I think that covers it pretty well!"

"It's interesting," Frank pointed out, "that you said 'people.' You include homosexuals in that statement?"

Jean tensed, and felt that somehow everybody in the room knew about her; then she realized there was no way for them to know. She relaxed. She was about to say something when Mr. Brown commented on the subject.

"What about homosexuals? There's a real conversation piece. Is it morally right—or morally wrong—for two men or two women to have intimate relations?"

There was silence, and then Mrs. Carter puffed out her chest and said staunchly, "They're disgusting! They aren't *human!*"

"Now what makes you think that?" Brown inquired politely.

"Well, what is sex for—if not to have children?"

Brown laughed. "I'll not answer that question directly, but I *will* suggest a question for each of you to ask yourselves, without needing to give a spoken answer. *How many times have you had sexual relations without the idea of having children? I'm talking about the pleasure factor. Bisexuality would fall into that, and homosexuality, along with pure heterosexuality.*"

Frank interjected with. "That's not the point, is it?"

"Isn't it? Look at it this way," Brown countered, pointing his finger at Frank. "Sex is physical, and it is a…well, brought down to the simplicity of it all—it's merely touching and being touched. Nerve endings, which respond to touch. Do you think the nerves know if the touch is male or female? Do you think that your muscles can tell that you're being touched by man or woman? Isn't sex merely physical pleasure brought to the point where it is almost pain and sometimes mixed with a certain amount of pain?"

Somebody said: "It's all in the head, anyway!"

Jean listened to the conversation with sinking depression. It seemed as if it were carried on for her benefit.

"I don't know," Frank admitted. "The idea of having physical relations, no matter how *innocent* my mind is to it, with a man—repels me! I don't think I could stand a woman that had made love to another woman—but then, I don't think I'd ever ask such a woman out. You can smell them a mile away!"

It was Jean's turn to explode into the argument. "How can you tell? What sign post, if any, is there? Do homosexuals have a neon sign flashing in front of them, telling the world what they are? Or is it that they have five arms, or three legs? Are they ugly? Are they...what *right* do you have to make such a statement? There's—you don't even know—we don't even know what we are talking about. Have you ever *seen* a Lesbian? Do you know what they are like? How they think? Do you have some idea that they are 'different'—so different that you can 'smell' them?"

There was a heavy, awkward silence. Her words had been filled with heated emotion, and suddenly she was afraid that in her statement she'd made the mistake of revealing her own hidden secret.

"I'm sorry but in New York I knew a woman that was a Lesbian and I don't think you could have 'smelled' her out no matter how much experience *you* had!" Her last words were directed at Frank. Then daringly she added, hoping that by coming out and suggesting it, the others could never believe it possible, "How do you know that I'm not a Lesbian?"

Frank laughed.

Mary cried, "Don't be silly! You're as normal as everybody else here!"

"What's normal?" Jean demanded, pushing her advantage.

Somebody said: "And what about bisexuals?"

That question remained unanswered.

"Where do you draw the line?" Jean continued. "I understand that the law states—that is, if you want to follow all the laws in all the states at once that the only way it is *legal* to have any relations with somebody of the opposite sex is to be married to them, with the man on top and the shades drawn, and only in the evening, for the sole purpose of having a baby. Only lip kissing and the act itself!"

Her brazen statement stilted the atmosphere as if she had dropped a rank smelling bomb in the middle of the room. Embarrassment settled over everybody and suddenly Jean wanted to just disappear, fade away to nothing. The conversation had gone too far, become too intimate and then been blasted with her final statements that had brought it down to bold, coldly stated facts, without any of the necessary social niceties.

Joe started to stand, nervously, and then asked if anybody wanted a drink.

"Oh, sit down!" Mary snapped angrily.

"You certainly slapped that one down!" Frank admitted a little later. "Where now?"

Mary laughed, high pitched. "That seems to have ended *that* topic of conversation—and fast!"

The others laughed lightly and then after a short silence started talking again, but this time in small groups of two or three. Jean was somehow left alone, not because anybody was trying to ignore her, but merely because what was being said by those talking directly around her weren't subjects on which she wished to converse. In a way she was glad to be momentarily ignored. For a long time she sat thinking about what she had said, wondering why she'd been so coldly biting. Then she shrugged off her uneasiness, forcing herself to accept her blunder as merely a normal mistake that overtakes people in the heat of an argument. No doubt the others were already beginning to forget, and there wasn't any reason she should suffer.

Jean was glad when the party finally came to a slow grinding end with the couples leaving one at a time. The Browns were last to go and Frank Martin left with them, shaking hands with Jean and reminding her that he would pick her up at the agreed upon time.

When the door had closed behind the guests, Mary turned to Jean and asked, "What was that all about?"

"What?"

"You have a date with Frank?"

"Oh, that. What of it?"

Mary smiled warmly. "Nothing. I'm glad. I was hoping that the two of you would like each other. That's why I had him over this evening."

"I know. It was thoughtful," Jean commented politely. Inwardly, she wished that her sister hadn't bothered. Yet there was the knowledge that it was no doubt the best thing for her. If she wanted to know about herself, the only possible way was letting a man become intimate with her. Frank Martin seemed as good as any. Even if he could "smell" a Lesbian! It might be a joy to poke that fact in his face, after having enjoyed a wild evening of sex.

A little later when Jean found the privacy of her

45

room, confused thoughts were raging through her
mind. She couldn't understand why it was possible
for her to accept so calmly the idea of letting Frank
seduce her. Before she had gone to New York she
had sworn never again to be an easy make for a
man. The affair with Al Gordon had left her with
bitter hatred toward the male sex. Now she was
quite calmly planning to allow another to seduce
her.

Jean bit on her lower lip, annoyed by those
thoughts, because no matter how she tried, it was
difficult to think of sex as something beautiful and
loving.

Love hadn't counted for three years.

Well, not the so-called "normal" love between a
man and woman. What she'd had been Debra was
something different; it involved affection and a kind
of love, but not in any way the same kind of romantic love that should be shared with the opposite sex.
She recognized that Debra had experienced deep
feelings for her, but Jean had never felt anything but
profound friendship for the other woman.

Sighing, Jean got carefully undressed and then
slipped into bed, naked. For a long time she lay
there thinking, but after a while gave up trying to
sort out her thoughts. Rolling tiredly over on her
side, Jean closed her eyes.

It was a long time before sleep finally began to
settle over her anguished thoughts. She never knew
when reality ended and dreams began.

*"Wake up," a man's voice whispered in her
ear. "Wake up, my pet!"*

*For several seconds Jean didn't move, she lay in
the ocean of her deep wonderful sleep, not wanting*

to move. It was the touch of the man's hands, which caused her to tense, startled.

Fingers were touching her breasts!

"What the damned hell are you doing?" she yelled, sitting up, angrily.

"Why, caressing your breasts, my pet!" Frank Martin stated quite matter-of-factly. "Can't you tell that?"

"Oh, go to hell! What right do you have to—?"

"Don't be silly," he whispered, leering down at her. "You gave me the right!"

His hands kept caressing her. "You know it's a man you want. Not a woman!"

"Please!"

"Don't please me!" he cursed, biting her ear-lobe. "I take what 1 want!"

Then suddenly he was forcing his body against hers.

Oh, Debra where are you?

Far away in New York! That's where you are. Out of my life!

She felt Frank surge down against her, driving at her body. Nausea flooded over her, she was bathing in sick hot sweat.

Suddenly, Jean realized she was sitting up in bed, screaming!

She heard footsteps in the hallway outside her room.

"What's wrong?" Mary's voice called through the door.

For a moment Jean didn't say anything, because her voice was captured somewhere deep inside her throat and didn't want to escape. Then finally a choking sound formed words. "Just a dream.

Sorry!"

She took a deep breath and then added, "I'm all right."

"You gave us a scare. I'll see you tomorrow, then. Goodnight." Mary's voice was heavily laden with concern.

"Goodnight," Jean called weakly back.

For a long time she lay there in bed, afraid to find sleep again, puzzling over the horrible dream, which had brought her sitting up, screaming.

It was well past four in the morning before she finally slipped back into unconsciousness. Pure exhaustion gave her dreamless sleep. When she woke late in the morning, her body felt more tired than it had when she'd gone to bed, her mind was still desperately confused and concerned about the dreams which had startled her awake. She lay in bed for a long time before getting up to face the new day.

The hours that followed were a blundering series of boring actions. She helped cleaning up after the party, and she had lunch in town with her sister. Later in the afternoon she took a long walk, alone. But her thoughts continued to remain unsettled, confused. It was important to find a job and a place of her own; that much she knew for certain. For the moment, though, it would be necessary to stay put until things could be arranged and that would take time.

That night she dreamed again. This time it was more horrifying than before.

A cloudless void surrounded her and she was drifting through a dimness of space which had no up and no down, no left or right, no front or back—just emptiness which stretched out as far as she could

48

see.

Then suddenly this void became alive with shape and color. Breasts were surrounding her on every side. Large ones, which were fully shaped like rounded mountains. Small ones, which were hardly more than large rosy nipples. Pulled and drooped ones. And at the ends, like little black drops, were men hanging from the erect nipples, dangling in a frantic fear that they might lose their grip and fall down into the burning, bubbling pit of lava far below. Then she felt a nibbling on her breasts and looked down in horror. There was a little man on the end of each of her breasts, squeezing tightly with their hands. They were like little grotesque human insects and she struck insanely at them. They fell down into the boiling lava below and then slowly disappeared, screaming in pain. She watched with an inner feeling of complete satisfaction. Then suddenly there were two more nibbling men. Her eyes returned to her breasts. They were now bleeding. A man was on each one, hacking away with a tiny broad hatchet.

She struck at them, but couldn't knock them off. Then she saw their features.

They were twins. Twin Frank Martins. Both laughed mockingly at her. "Now what do you think? You can't kill men—you can't get rid of your desires for men by killing them off. But I'm fixing you! Fixing you...good!"

Suddenly there was a large male form on hers and now the voice was coming from his lips, which were right next to her ear. "You want a man, don't you? You want a man very much! You want me!"

"No, no. I want Debra. I want Debra! Nobody

else! Just Debbie!" she sobbed *frantically, desperately, pleadingly. "Just Debra!"*

Abruptly she was sitting up in bed, clutching at her breasts and saying in a low whisper over and over again, "I want Debbie. I want Debbie."

It was several moments before Jean realized that she was awake and that it was now morning. For a long time she sat there, her eyes clamped tightly shut, and then suddenly she choked out the disgust inside her. After a while, Jean lay back and attempted to soothe her tormented thoughts and nerves. Every muscle ached from the tension of the dream.

What was wrong, that she should be having such nightmares? she wondered silently.

Never in her life had such dreams plagued her sleep. It terrified Jean.

"And I don't *want Debbie!"* she moaned softly. "I don't want her! I want a husband and children!" She clutched at her sides, her whole body shaking. "I want to be normal. I want a home and a normal life."

After a few moments she added, more calm now, "Goddamn Debra Channings. And damn men, too. And sex." But there was almost a half-hidden tone of humor to her voice.

After a while, Jean got up from bed and went into the half-bath, showered, and then dressed in pedal pushers. But she didn't leave her room, instead, she lay on the bed, smoking and trying to reason out the terrible, haunting nightmare.

Chapter Four

Sitting in the dimness of the seaside restaurant, watching the ocean waves break on the shore, had a soothing effect on Jean's shattered nerves. The last three nights with their terrible nightmares had created an edgy nervousness towards the prospect of actually having the date with Frank Martin.

But here she was with him.

Now looking from the ocean to the quiet strength of the man's face caused her to feel a new confidence. Frank was a nice man, the kind of person with whom a girl could enjoy herself, without the fear of being taken advantage of, unless this was what she wanted. That awareness seemed strange, considering the fact that no doubt he was interested in more than mere friendship with a female.

"You've been sitting there thinking for a long time," Frank commented in a low, rich voice. "You haven't even touched your lobster!"

"I'm sorry, Frank. I got to thinking. I'm really enjoying myself. I can't tell you how much. It's been a long time since I've felt so relaxed and comfortable." She finished the statement in her mind: a *long time since I've been out with a man.*

"Like I told you, things are different since you left L.A."

Jean smiled silently and thought: *if he only knew!*

Jean carefully began picking at her lobster. On the menu it had sounded more inviting than it looked on her plate. *Broiled Australian lobster tail, drawn butter.* It tasted good enough, but it wasn't the *food* that she was concerned with. Her mind was occupied with what was sure to happen later in the evening. Would Frank take her to his apartment, to a motel or...where? Or maybe he wouldn't even make a pass at her. And then, maybe he would and she might end up negating such an idea. Pass and parry.

Sipping her stinger cocktail, Jean let the liquor rest in her mouth for a while and then slowly swallowed it. The drink was strong, but didn't have any real effect on her. At first she had felt a light numbness, but it was now beginning to wear thin.

"I was wondering," Frank said, "if you have any plans for next weekend."

"Boy, you're really giving me the rush job, aren't you!" Jean laughed self-consciously. But it flattered and pleased her.

"Not really. Just that you're an attractive woman, intelligent, lovely company and—"

"Don't tell me that you don't know other women—at least as attractive as myself—maybe even more so."

"Pumping for compliments?" he teased.

"No. Not really. Just...wondering."

"Nothing to wonder about. I date. I do so with a number of nice ladies," Frank admitted, a twinkle in his eyes. "Though no more desirable than you are. But let's say I find you holding my attention—for the present, at least."

52

"That sounds ominous." She couldn't help smiling.

"Sorry, it wasn't supposed to." He took a bite of his New York steak. "Well, how about it?"

"I don't know. Everything is up in the air. I don't know really what I plan on doing—maybe getting a job here in L.A. and then an apartment. I don't think I should stay too long at Mary's."

"What do you do?"

"Secretary." Her fork nibbled on the last piece of lobster.

"Any good?"

Red flushed her cheeks. "I believe so. Good references, anyway."

"That always helps."

"Well, I conned them into believing I knew what I was doing. Nobody can be as good as I appear to be on paper."

"Hmmm…interesting. A paper secretary?"

"Something like that. And some typing, too."

"Fast?"

"Well, I do as many as ten words a minute. Is that impressive enough?"

"Amazing. At that speed you'd be almost able to keep up with my dictation. I do about eleven words a minute!"

"Then, alas, I assume you won't be hiring me!"

"Hiring you, as what?"

"Well, a secretary, of course. Why else do you think I accepted your offer of dinner?"

"My, my. You sure are getting on the wild side. Real *risqué*!"

"*Risqué*?" she countered, with a teasing wink. "What in the world does that mean?"

"Well, it is French for dirt-táy…but you are certainly beautifully pure white clean to the core."

"You never can tell about us women, can you?" Then as if shocked at what she'd said: "Oh, I didn't quite mean it exactly that way."

"I suppose not."

"What will you think of me now?"

"What would you like me to think?"

"Well, something nice, I suppose."

The both laughed at that, then after a short silence, while rather thoughtfully studying her, he said: "My company could use a woman like you. You're good for business."

"You offering me a job?" she questioned, taking another sip of the stinger.

"We *could* use a good secretary. Good ones are hard to find. We do have a number of positions offered."

"Now that does sound…what's the word you used? Oh, yes, *risqué!*"

"Not at all. I'm serious." His eyes turned up, looking into Jean's.

"Heaven forbid that you'd be serious this soon in our relationship!"

"I mean about the job." He smiled softly at that, took her hand in his, but said: "If you decide you want a job—consider me, first. Promise?"

"Okay. If you say so."

She was actually enjoying the man, and the verbal exchange. He had a quick wit and was quite playful, even while at the same time offering a light element of seriousness here and there. She felt comfortable with him.

It was good to be away from the Hanson house

for an evening, Jean thought. There had been continued little arguments which took place between her sister and Joe, and she couldn't forget the strange glances the man kept giving her when he thought she wasn't looking. It was unsettling. It was one of those awkward situations Jean wanted to avoid.

"There you go thinking again," Frank's voice cut off her thoughts.

"Sorry. I got to wondering about Joe and Mary." For a moment she hesitated and then decided that it probably wouldn't be talking out of turn to ask Frank what he thought about the marriage, because he probably knew more about it than she did. "Do you think they're…well, happy?"

Frank's face grew serious as he asked, "Do you want to know the truth?"

Jean nodded, tensing inwardly.

Frank said, "No. They aren't."

It hung there for several seconds until she asked him to continue.

"I don't know…well that's not true. Joe talks a lot to me about his…problems. They're very much in love with each other, there's no question about that part of it otherwise they wouldn't have lasted past the honeymoon. Your sister—now don't get mad about my saying this, but your sister is…frigid."

A chill rushed down Jean's spine. A tight hand squeezed at the pit of her stomach. For some reason his statement was as unnerving as if he had said, *Jean, you're a Lesbian!*

It seemed terribly cold of Frank to have come right out and said it in that way. It was also a bit irritating, hearing it from Frank. Her tone of voice instinctively indicated her irritation when she said. "How do *you* know?"

"It's no secret that they don't get along sexually. She lets him make love to her but, well, to be truthful, *no* man likes it when a woman just *lets* him make love to her. He wants to give her pleasure. Joe loves Mary very much, but what can he do?"

"Maybe we shouldn't be talking about it," Jean suggested tightly.

"We shouldn't—but now that you've brought it up...maybe I could say something to you. If Mary could—well, *act* like she likes it—that would help."

"Thanks. But I'm not the one to tell her that."

"Why?"

"Because we haven't been *that* close since we were children. We lived our own lives. She wanted a family and to settle down. She's what I call the backyard gossip type. She doesn't gossip—but that's just as far as her mental ability goes. I wanted to go out in the world and she just wanted her own little home and family—I'm not saying I don't want a family, someday, but Mary didn't want to wait. And that's really all she seemed to want in order to fulfill her needs. Well, she's gotten part of it..."

"If the time ever comes around, it might do a lot of good if you tried to tell her." Frank was silent for a few minutes and then finally added, almost as an afterthought, "A man can be easily fooled, sometimes especially when he's in love."

That exchange was a damper.

The conversation lagged after that. When dinner was finished they had a couple of cocktails and then, around ten-thirty, left the restaurant. They drove along the beach highway to a small club

56

where there was three-piece combo that played dance music.

While they sat sipping martinis, Jean found her thoughts returning to her own personal problems and the fact that the people surrounding her were so much involved with their own tragic lives that they didn't have time to really be interested or concerned about her. A stab of self-pity moved through her. She felt suddenly alone and helpless.

"Want to dance?" Frank finally asked, after a long silence.

They danced for some time and the rhythm of the music and the nearness of the man against Jean caused her to feel a sudden detached desire to rediscover a man. She felt almost impersonal about it. Not that she didn't like Frank as a person, nor find him unattractive as a man. She literally didn't really know how she felt about him as a lover. To her, the moment, the immediate situation offered a solution to nagging doubt about her own sexuality. Here was a man who would take simple pleasure out of making love to her. He might even be nice and gentle. But all of that was of little importance, a side issue. The fact was here she had a simple way to start rediscovering herself. She had to start somewhere; and the sooner the better.

It was this wanting, plus the sudden strong, numbing effects of the martini, which caused her to impulsively whisper softly into Frank's ear.

"Can't we go someplace?"

The man tensed and then pressed her tighter to him. "1 didn't want to push things too fast"

"Would it be?" she wondered, almost to herself.

He hesitated and then said, "That depends."

"You mean you're turning down my offer?" she laughed, yet sounded somewhat defensive.

"Hell, no! I'm just a little...well, surprised—"

"Disappointed in me? Is that what you were thinking?" The drinks and the desire had completely melted all guilt or pride. She just didn't give a damn. It didn't matter if this man thought she was just a little tramp or not. He was merely a symbol, a stud who could prove to her that she still liked sex with men. Suddenly she didn't want to wait any longer, playing this socially polite game, when both of them realized where they would probably end up before the evening was over. If he thought she was cheap because of it that didn't really matter.

"I'm not disappointed. Who would be? Any man in his right mind would go out of his way to have a woman like you." Frank hesitated, and then laughed briefly. "I'd have thought it might have taken at least a couple more hours, that's all."

"You're a slob!" Jean whispered, half kidding, half serious.

They finished the dance and then went to their table. He paid the bill and they left. Once in the car, Frank turned to her. "You weren't kidding? You were serious?"

"I don't kid about such things, Frank," she told him, levelly.

"Okay, then. Want to stop off for a bottle?"

"No."

They drove in silence for a long time and Jean had the feeling that she had made a mistake in offering to let him take her to a motel.

Why should you care what he thinks about you? You came to L.A. to do just this, the moment you got the chance even if you didn't put it quite that way.

Frank pulled the car up to the front of a large motel and then killed the engine. "I'll be back in a moment." He got out and disappeared into the doorway marked "Office."

Jean sat there listening to the night sounds around her. The beach behind the car was a soft melody of rippling, dancing water. There was a salt smell and taste to the air, which seemed crystal clear to her lungs. Everything was new and wonderful. Alive. Suddenly, her pulse was racing and she felt her heart pounding inside her heaving chest. It had happened so fast that she hadn't had time to really get used to the idea to react physically, emotionally, or even mentally, until now.

It seemed like hours before Frank opened the door of the office and stepped toward the car. He opened the car door and helped Jean out. "We have Room 4-E—down that way." He pointed toward the far side of the motel, away from the office.

They walked silently toward the end of the building. Jean's thoughts were racing like a frantic hurricane.

What's he thinking...and why did I let myself be the one to suggest it? Will this be the beginning and the end of Frank Martin? And what difference does it make? You're acting like a schoolgirl—why didn't you say "Yes" when he offered to buy a bottle?

"Frank?"

"Yes?" he asked, fitting the key to the door of Room 4-E.

"Could I ask a favor?"

"What?"

"You won't mind?"

"That depends," he laughed. "You sound so serious."

"I hope you won't be mad."

"You mean you've decided this is a mistake?" His voice was tight, but more in concern—honestly concerned.

"No. Oh, nothing like that. I just discovered I *could* use a drink."

"Is that all?" Frank laughed and then opened the door. "Go on in and I'll get something. Anything special?"

"No. Anything you like," she told him as he started to move away. "Oh, by the way. You have a cigarette?"

He returned and handed her a. pack and some matches. "I'll get more—glad you asked." He smiled down at her and for a moment they stared at each other. Then without any warning he lowered his lips and for a few seconds they pressed softly to Jean's mouth. Then he was gone.

Jean stood there at the door, watching him walk to the car, get in and drive away. The kiss was the first she had received from a man for a very long time. It seemed strangely different—and nicely pleasant. Finally she turned and stepped into the motel room and closed the door behind her.

Sitting on the large double bed, Jean pulled out a cigarette from the pack Frank had given her and lighted it. For several minutes she dragged deeply on the little white cylinder, trying not to think about the next hour, trying to clear her mind of the fear and nervousness aching through every muscle in her body.

You're acting like a damned virgin prude on her

first affair! she scolded herself.

Yet, in a way, it was much like that, Jean realized. With Al Gordon, three years before, it had been more than just an affair; it had been a loving romance—at least from her viewpoint. And because of that element it hadn't seemed like just a sordid affair, like the one that was now developing between Frank and herself. She had been in love with Al Gordon, while she didn't really care much one way or another—seriously—about Frank.

Al had been the man she was employed by and they had gone out many times on business dinners together. It was such an old story that it embarrassed her to think about it. Secretary falls in love with "playboy" boss. Only, Al hadn't been quite a playboy, but she had thought of him as a misunderstood husband. And Al had played it like a symphony into her ears, letting her hum the melody of his lies over and over until all she could think about was that wonderful moment when he would get his divorce and marry her. Then the *affair.* It had developed so slowly, so carefully, that she hadn't even realized when it had actually started within her mind. It was developing and already an event within her consciousness when he first took her to a motel. That night, when her virginity had been taken, had become a strange memory for Jean. It was the first moment when she had become fully aware of being a woman; also the first time when her love had been misused.

And *how* it had been cheapened and used.

She had responded to his touches. The first kiss was a body embrace, with both of them fully clothed. She was gasping as one of his hands went around to the back of her dress and pulled down the zipper, caressingly. She'd clung to him as he slowly glided his hands along her back, fingers sending electric charges over her naked flesh. Then with amazing skill he'd unlatched the bra and a moment later was slipping the dress top and bra off her shoulders.

"They're beautiful!" he'd half moaned. Then led her to the bed.

With skilled hands he stripped her body naked.

"Oh, Al," she half sobbed, "you feel so good!"

He had made gentle love to her, taking his time, making it last for what seemed an eternity.

The man had been an excellent, tender lover; just a shit as a human being.

Jean's thoughts returned to the present. Her eyes examined the room.

It was small, modernly furnished, with a large television set opposite the bed. *They could turn it on a blank channel,* she thought, *and dim it so there would be the flood of make-believe moonlight bathing over their nude bodies.*

Standing, Jean stepped to the set, turned it on, and waited until it had warmed up. After a few moments she worked with the dials until the lighting was just right to give the "moonlight" effect she desired.

Stepping to the washroom, she removed her clothes, just leaving on her bra and panties, and then folded the dress, put it on a chair in the other room, and stepped to the bed. She pulled down the covers, and slid under them.

It seemed funny to Jean that it didn't feel strange anymore, being in a motel, planning on sexual relations with a man she had only met a few days before.

It should seem strange, she realized. It would have been completely out of the question before she had left for New York, but a lot of things had happened to her since then. She'd changed, matured in many ways, hardened.

Jean wondered what kind of lover Frank would turn out to be: the forceful kind that yanked you into his arms, not caring if you enjoyed it or not; the savage, brutal male animal that took and demanded; or the gentle lover that bathed your body with kisses and caresses until you were wild with desperation for him to become a part of you.

A lover like Debra had been.

She ripped her thoughts away from Debbie. *I don't want to think about her!*

She forced the image of Frank into her mind, reliving the lingering feel of his body moving against hers as they had danced the evening away. That had almost been ecstatic.

For a long time Jean lay there thinking, half dreaming, wondering if Frank could prove to her that she still was a real woman with normal female desires and passions. A half sleep finally settled over her mind and she wasn't aware of the door opening and Frank stepping into the room; it wasn't until the man's lips touched hers that she was startled awake.

"Oh, I didn't hear you—I'm sorry. I drifted off," she explained, quickly sitting up, forgetting her semi-nudity.

Frank looked at her in open admiration.

"You really *are* beautiful!" he whispered in a

low and husky voice. His eyes hungrily took in the swells of her breasts and the deep valley between their full fleshy mountains. Then he jerked his eyes away and looked at the television set. "I see you've set the mood and everything up already."

"Don't you approve?"

"Sure do. You're quite a woman, Jean. Full of such wonderful surprises!"

She laughed self-consciously. "How about that drink?"

"Coming up."

She watched him stepping into the bathroom and returning with two water glasses.

"I hope you don't mind straight booze."

"No."

He pulled out a pint of whiskey and opened it. Then, after pouring several shots into each glass, he came over to the bed and sat down next to Jean.

"Here you are!" he saluted, handing over a glass.

Jean thankfully sipped the whiskey. The liquor of the evening seemed to have worn completely off, the glow and the excitement of raw sexual need had dulled. She felt the demand for that "to hell with the world" attitude which had been so vivid while they were dancing.

"You're a strange girl, Jean," Frank commented, eyeing her breasts, whose shape he could easily see the proof of, though whose complete form was still hidden under the tight bra.

"What makes you say that?" Jean swallowed another large gulp of the whiskey, feeling a hard burn as it settled down into her stomach.

"Well, let's put it this way; you're different than

I would've thought."

"Again—in what way?" The liquor was finally beginning to work its slow way to her brain.

"Well, you seemed...well, cold, at first. What I mean is, you didn't warm up to me. Then *this* evening, I guess it's surprised me."

"A girl has the right to change her mind, doesn't she?"

"That's the way the book tells it. But I've found it doesn't always work that way."

"How *does* it work—usually?" Jean asked, mildly interested. She was much more concerned about delaying matters until the alcoholic haze had formed around her mind.

"Well, usually you can tell about a woman." He was avoiding the question.

Jean finished her drink and indicated with her eyes that she wanted some more.

Frank got up and returned with her glass. "That should keep you."

"I should *hope* so!" she exclaimed, laughing.

She was thoughtful as her lips sipped on the whiskey. "Tell me, Frank, what kind of girls do you usually go out with?"

"All kinds." Again his voice showed that he was avoiding a direct answer.

Jean pushed the point. "Even virgins?"

Frank's expression frowned, seriously. "No, I don't believe a gentleman should take a virgin out with any purpose other than being serious. I don't believe in seducing virgins."

"Then you only take out women you *can* seduce?" She couldn't help a biting addition of: "You must be pretty sure of me! What makes you think

65

I'm not a virgin?"

He seemed startled by her question. For a moment he didn't find an answer; then finally he stumbled over an explanation. "What I mean is, a man will take a woman out that he…well if he is interested in such things…a woman that might be willing to go into a more mature relationship because she's adult enough to handle it.

"What I'm saying is, what takes place—well, like you said the other day: what takes place between a man and a woman is nobody's business except the two involved. If a woman is adult and has had affairs and isn't *against* having them, then there's no reason why a man should turn down her gift of love."

"That doesn't actually explain what I asked."

"I guess not." Frank smiled and then leaned closer to her; his lips brushed her cheeks. "Why talk about such things?"

"Why not?" she turned and looked evenly into his eyes, unblinking.

"Okay, then. I'll bring it to a quick and *complete* end. I'm interested in women that aren't afraid of sex and are not afraid to act like *women.* Women who will be willing to have an affair with me, if things work out in that way. It's a little awkward to be with a girl who's afraid. When a situation comes about which could be developed into an intimate relationship and she chickens out. That's no fun for the man or the woman. A mature man looks for mature *women* to be with. In my case, I don't have the time to waste on children—let other men teach them how to grow up. I'm not a School of Love!"

The heat and force of his words and the burning

look in his eyes had stripped away the romantic mood. They sat there for a long time without saying anything. Then slowly Frank's hand moved to her leg, which was still under the covers, and gently caressed it.

"You're okay, Jean. Let's just not talk about that subject any more. I don't like it and I don't think it's nice to talk about other women—or the way I might be with them—with the woman I'm with at the moment. It's not very subtle or romantic or flattering."

They were silent a little while longer after that, his fingers idly caressing her leg, and slowly rebuilding the intimate mood.

Both of them seemed to want to recharge their mutual desire, to somehow get past the immediate conversational impasse.

Jean sipped her drink until it was finished. The liquor had finally begun to form the haze around her mind.

"Frank—I'm sorry I forced the subject. You're really quite a nice guy." She meant it. Her eyes flowed along his body, and the desire to be a more intimate was already beginning to ripen an intense hunger. It seemed strange being with a man after so long a time, but she was now eager to discover how her body would react.

Frank's eyes turned toward Jean, and in the dim television "moonlight" his features seemed hard and chiseled.

Yet there was a small voice in the back of her mind that screamed: *Will he give me pleasure? Really?*

Jean felt Frank's hand move up her leg and she

liked the way her nerves responded. Slowly, so slowly, in fact, that she wasn't even aware it was happening. He gently planted a gentle kiss on her lips, then lowered her back down onto the bed, saying, "You are beautiful, Jean!"

Then he covered her lips again, though it was a gentle, closed-mouth kiss of tenderness, but still fully rewarding.

It lingered for a moment and then he slipped away from the bed. Her eyes were closed and she was only aware of the sound of movement, the sound of clothing falling to the floor. Then suddenly Frank's form moved down to hers. She felt his hands slide the covers from her body and then subtly move over her stomach and across her thighs. This time, when his lips touched hers they were parted and the tip of his tongue ran along the surface of her mouth. She opened her lips to him and felt the stab of wonderful pleasure.

Somehow, during the embrace, Frank's hands circled her body and his fingers moved skillfully, unclasping her bra and working it off her breasts. It disappeared from existence and she felt his lips slide over her throat, along her shoulder, and finally glide toward a fully erect nipple. It lingered for only a moment before seeking out the rigid mate.

Jean felt wonderful excitement float through her; a frantic joy and happiness waved over her mind at the mere knowledge that her body was responding so completely to his caresses.

She gloried in his touch, his kisses, as he tongued over her body like a musician working over his instrument with skill and care, as if he were playing a sensitive, complicated concert. Each touch

68

and each sensation became another note in the melodic composition of his love-making, each building logically to the next note, each rising to a crescendo and then dropping slightly back, never completely releasing the tension, merely giving momentarily a minor rest before the next wonderful upward swing of pleasure attacked her nerves. Wave upon wave ran smoothly through her body until pleasure was beginning to become a storm, gentle at first and then slowly more and more demanding and forceful, as the last movement of his concerto of love came into being.

The storm suddenly raged into a hurricane as his body drove down against hers with a terrible violence which consumed all thoughts, all awareness except that of being whipped by passion-winds, tossed toward the tormented shore, against the rocks of pain and pleasure, each time to be driven back into the enveloping ocean, only to be once more slashed against the rocks until she cried out in the anguish, pleading, begging for the final release which only her own body was holding back.

Jean's mind became a numbed thing captured inside the cavity of her skull, unable to do anything but insanely wait until the storm had passed. She felt that the release would never come, and then, as skillfully as it had begun, she felt herself lifted one time more toward those jagged rocks, to finally shoot past onto the shore, exhausted, spent, joyously relieved by the ecstasy of pure pleasure which had finally covered over her nerves and smashed her to the safety of completion.

For a long time she lay there unable to move, unable to think or respond to the wonderful pleasure which had convulsed through her; unable to think about the man who had just given it to her; unable to wonder about herself and how it was possible for her to enjoy a man and at the same time enjoy a woman; unable to wonder what kind of human animal her body was; unable to even care about wondering.

Then slowly, the thoughts began to take form, but, at first, without any organization or shape.

Then she saw:

Debra Channings and her lovely body, naked and waiting, standing in the darkness. Looking down at her, watching.

The mental image of her Lesbian lover jarred away the picture of pleasure that Frank's body had given. Jean felt herself go tense inside, felt herself numb with guilt and mental pain. *Oh, Debbie—I'm sorry—please forgive me!*

Frantically she tore the thought away. She sat up, opening her eyes. Frank was sitting next to her, looking at the far wall.

"You're wonderful, Jean. The most wonderful woman I've ever known. Don't ask me why I feel this way—and don't think I'm giving a line which I've told other girls."

"Stop!" she choked out, anguished.

Her mind was wild with pained confusion, fear and terror. The only thing she wanted was escape, to run from her thoughts, to escape from the torment that was now possessing her mind.

"I don't want to talk!" she reached for Frank and savagely pressed against him. The feel of his hairy, flat, man's chest was strange compared to memory of Debra and the largeness of the woman's breasts

70

pushing against her own breasts.

"I don't want to think!" she sobbed in desperation. "Make me stop thinking!"

"What's wrong?" Frank wanted to know.

"Please...just love me...let me love you!" she pleaded, clutching tighter against the man.

In desperation she parted her thighs, rolled over on top of him, then started tonguing his chest, nipples, then over the flat hardness of his muscular stomach, and then lower. She didn't want to stop. It was the most thrillingly crazy experience she'd ever known.

She kept thinking how different this was from the dildo Debra had used. They had both playfully mouthed the thing many times while the other was orally having a Lesbian feast.

But Frank was actively responsive to the kisses.

With a moan, she released him, and repositioned herself so it would be possible to let him enter her, penetrate deeply.

He reached out, cupped her breasts, squeezed, fondled, and gently stroked fingers across her nipples as she continued to surge against him.

"Oh, you're wonderful!" she sobbed, thrilling. *I'm hot for him!*

It was the very unladylike manner in which the thought formed itself that caused her to respond physically. She lifted up, then plunged down, totally enveloping him, sobbing at the pleasure she experienced.

"God, Jean!" he exclaimed between tortured, tense lips.

She merely moaned, thrilling to every rapid penetration.

It lasted longer than she had expected and when the flood of his orgasm burst deep within her, Jean climaxed, too.

Taking command like she had, thrilled Jean far more than she could have thought possible.

But a little later, after cigarettes and little conversation, the memory of Debra tore at her guts and she was suddenly pleading for Frank to smother her with erotic kisses, and wonderful caresses that could once more bring escape from her anguished thoughts.

For a moment Frank didn't move, and then he slowly lowered Jean back on the bed and covered her lips with his.

They kissed for a long time, but there wasn't any of the desperation that had been present before; this time Jean was fully aware of what was happening, aware of the things that were different in his lovemaking. The harder hands, the rougher lips, the steel flatness of his chest.

She tried, she moved her body against his; she squirmed as he joined her; she thought about the pleasure which his actions had given a little while before; she strained up against his body, aware of the hardness of him.

But none of the pleasure returned, none of the wonderful ecstasy. This time it was merely an act that she played out, an action her body did in obedience to her mind. This time she lay back, her eyes closed, as he moved from her, bathed in guilt, bathed in the horror that no matter what she had tried to feel there had been nothing but numbed sensation, little feeling and even less pleasure.

What was wrong? her mind asked over and over

again, never finding the answer. *It had been good those first two times. Now she could only think of Debra.*

It wasn't until about four-thirty in the morning that they got up and dressed. Neither of them said anything, and Jean was terribly afraid that Frank had guessed what had happened during their last union. But he said nothing about it. He honored her silence.

All the way back to her sister's home they were quiet. It wasn't until he was standing at the door, on the porch, that he said anything.

"You were wonderful, Jean." But there was a hidden questioning in his voice and beyond the veiled surface of his eyes.

He had guessed that there was something wrong, Jean was sure of that, but she was also sure that he didn't know what.

"Thank you for a wonderful evening, Frank. You don't know how much it has meant to me." She smiled, but felt it was forced.

He took her hand in his and then leaned closer, caressing her mouth with his own. "I'll see you again?"

"Probably."

"About next weekend."

"Let it work out."

"I'll call you tomorrow?"

"That's fine." Jean turned and opened the door with the key Mary had loaned her.

Without another word she stepped into the house and closed the door behind her. Leaning back against it, Jean took a deep, tired breath and stood there for a long time, dazed.

What's wrong with you, Jean? she silently de-

73

manded. *You liked it the first two times. What happened?*

Slowly and quietly she moved through the darkened house to her room. Once the door had closed behind her she rushed to the bed and collapsed on it, sobbing. It wasn't until the sun was just beginning to creep over the horizon that sleep finally came to her emotionally exhausted body and mind.

Chapter Five

"Did you enjoy yourself with Frank last night?" Mary asked over the lunch table. They were in a small Mexican restaurant, eating Beef Enchiladas and Chiles Rellenos.

"He's a nice man," Jean answered, fighting a mental battle to keep from screaming at Mary to keep quiet *about* the date with Frank.

The dreams which had followed woke her at eleven-thirty that morning, but were still vivid in her mind. That world of breasts had returned to plague her rest, that horrid nightmare of the little insect Franks hacking at her breasts.

"More salsa, *señoritas*?" their waiter Miguel asked.

She waved him off. She didn't want to think about the dream or Frank—or even the salsa. Not then, anyway. It was all too confused in her mind.

"That doesn't answer my question," Mary pointed out, her voice thick with interest.

"I don't want to talk about it right now." Jean snapped, angrily.

"Did he *try* something with you?" Mary's face froze in shocked hardness.

"Oh, it's nothing like that! I just don't want to talk about last night. Can't we talk about something else?"

They were silent for a while and then Mary, after taking a last bite of the chile relleno, looked up at Jean and asked, "What're your plans?"

"I don't know. I think maybe it would be a good idea to get a job right away, and then an apartment as soon as possible."

"Oh, don't be silly!" But Mary's voice sounded relieved.

"It would be better, Mary. After all, you have your own life to lead, you're still newly married and—"

"I don't think you're getting in the way of anything that we want to do!" Bitterness burned Mary's eyes. She looked blankly at her plate.

"Can't you do anything about that?" Jean inquired, remembering what Frank had told her.

"What?"

"I don't know. You might try fooling him. Fake it a little; every woman does, one time or another...well the smart ones, anyway."

Jean felt suddenly stupid, saying it, but it was a way to get the conversation off herself and onto something else.

"Are you kidding? You can't fool a man about *that!*" Mary exploded. Then suddenly she looked nervously around and said: "This isn't the place to be talking about such things."

There was silence for a while and then Mary once again broke it. "You know, I believe Joe could give you a job. He's overloaded with work that keeps him busy working late, and maybe he could use you."

"Frank offered me a job—but..." Jean hesitated,

and realized that Mary wasn't really as concerned about offering her a job as she was about the possibility of challenging Joe about his late hours. It was the kind of excuse men used too often, so often that it had become trite.

"I've gotta work late," they would say— meaning there was some girl they were working' with.

That had been the way it was with Al Gordon three years before.

Jean tore her mind from the past. "Well, maybe it *would* be nice to keep it in the family—if Joe could really use me."

"He better be able to—that's all I can—" Mary broke off, as if realizing the anger had revealed her actual purpose in suggesting that Joe might hire Jean. "What I mean—"

"Forget it. I'd be glad to work for Joe. It'd give me something to do. Already, the vacation's getting on my nerves."

Mary looked silently at Jean, her face pressed with honest concern. "You haven't been sleeping well, have you?"

"Bad dreams."

"I thought so. I've heard you cry out at night—"

Jean felt herself tense. "What'd *I* say?" She made the question seem casual and hoped her sister hadn't noticed the reaction on her face.

"Oh, I don't know. Nothing I can remember." Mary was lying, that much Jean felt sure of. "Anyway if something's bothering you I know a man who might help. Doctor Handle. He's the guy I've been going to. In my case—well, he says it's probably all in my mind—that I really would like it if I could get the fears out of my head." Mary stopped, her eyes darting around the almost empty room. "Let's get out of here. I don't want the whole world to know what's going on."

They finished their meal in silence, paid the bill and left. For the rest of the afternoon the conversation was general. They window-shopped along the Sunset Strip, looking at dresses and household things on Hollywood Boulevard. By five-thirty they returned home and Mary started fixing dinner. About ten minutes after they had arrived home the phone rang, and Jean felt herself go tense inside.

Is that Frank? she wondered nervously, biting her lower lip.

"If it's Frank, give some excuse. I'm tired—I don't want to talk to him right now." Immediately she wondered why she had said that.

Mary answered the phone. There was a long conversation and then her voice raised loud enough so that Jean could hear.

"Oh, go have your damned fun!"

The anger and bitterness expressed in those words jarred Jean. The receiver crashed down on the hook and silence followed.

Jean went to the kitchen and put an arm around Mary.

They stood there for a long time and then finally the older woman turned and said in a dead-sounding voice, "Joe's 'working.' Late, as usual."

Jean didn't argue the point, believing it would be better to let it alone. Yet she felt an inner desire to relieve Mary's guilt and fear, to somehow let the other woman know that she wasn't the only one tormented with such feelings, with such desperations.

Neither of them said anything for a long time, not until dinner was ready and they were sitting at the table, staring at the fried potatoes and hamburger steaks.

"Mary, don't think you're the only one caught in an emotional trap," Jean offered, gently.

"Oh. I'm not feeling sorry for myself!"

"That's not what I meant." Jean hesitated, unsure of what she wanted to say.

"Just what *did* you mean then?" There was an edge of probing anger to Mary's words.

"Just that…well, there are other problems worse than just *not* liking sex."

Mary's eyes flared up into Jean's, heavy with fury and pain. "Oh, now you're telling me my problem's nothing. I guess yours is so much worse?"

A stony silence froze over them.

Jean broke it. "That's not what I mean. You should know I'm trying to help."

"Oh, I know what you're thinking. *What's wrong with Mary? After all, she has a husband! She should he happy! What right does she have to complain?*"

The bitterness and anger and the hurt and pain suddenly burst over Jean, flooding her mind with so many conflicting emotions that, for a moment, she found it hard not to scream. Instead she said:

"What right do you have to talk to me that way? You don't even know the beginning of it all! Everything you wanted has worked out! If you aren't sexually normal, well, that's not *my* fault—and don't think things are so 'normal' with me, either. I have a *few* problems of my own. All our lives you got everything you wanted—everything *your* way! All you wanted was a home and a husband. Well, you have it! I had to go out and do things the hard way—work for what I got. You had it handed to you! So don't tell me where to get off!"

Jean's explosion had come so fast and so unexpectedly that both women sat there in stunned, shocked silence. Mary's face had drawn white, becoming coldly stiff.

Jean felt the horror of what she had said and wanted desperately to take every word back. Suddenly she found herself saying the very things she had sworn never to tell anybody.

"Forgive me. That's not what I mean. It's just that in New York I discovered something about myself that—that's so horrible I don't even like to think about it. All I can say is that it involves a woman and myself—*not* a man!"

Terror caught like a lump in Jean's throat as she realized what she'd done, and saw Mary's reaction. The implication hadn't been lost. What was more terrifying was that she had even said it at all.

Without a word, Jean stood and rushed from the room. Without knowing where she was going, she ran out of the house and down the street. It was a long time before she slowed down to a walk. Her breath was labored and hot in her lungs. Her whole body ached.

What made me say that to Mary? she screamed over and over again in her mind, clutching her hands into tight fists with every repetition of the question.

She couldn't stay at her sister's any longer, now. The disgust and horror would be in Mary's eyes

80

every time she looked at her; there would be the condemning with every glance and every subtle word.

Oh, God, you really made a mess of things this time, Jean!

Suddenly the urge to have a drink caused her mouth to become even dryer than it had been from the exercise of running. She was standing at Pico and Westwood, waiting for a red light to change, when she spotted a small cocktail lounge down the street. Stepping toward it, Jean determined to get herself roaring drunk, realizing that this was the only possible way she would face the next hours. Then, suddenly, she realized she didn't have any money with her. In the frantic escape from her sister, she had forgotten to get her purse. For a desperate instant Jean stood there on the sidewalk, undecided and unsure of herself. She didn't want to return to Mary. She didn't know Frank's phone number or where he worked, and didn't have a dime or twenty-five cents to pay for a phone call. But she *did* know where to find Joe Hanson. Her brother-in-law owned Hanson Trucking Agency, and it wasn't far from his home. All she had to do was look up the address in the telephone book.

She found and entered a phone booth. After a couple of minutes search, she found the listing she was looking for. *The Hanson Trucking Agency* was on Westwood Boulevard. She made a mental note of the address and started north on Westwood. There was a long walk ahead of her, well over twenty blocks. But that didn't really matter. She'd be able to get a loan from Joe—*if* he was around.

During the long walk Jean had time to think

more carefully about herself and what she had said to Mary. And time to wonder what insane inner drive had urged her to make such a confession. There hadn't been any logical reason for her to tell of her life in New York. And certainly not from the viewpoint of trying to "help" Mary. It didn't make sense, unless there had been an inner need to talk to somebody, no matter what the price, a subconscious, demanding pressure to get the confession off her chest. If she was Catholic she'd find a priest. But that was out of the question. The modern-day "priest" was the professional shrink. The confessional booth had been altered into a couch, which wasn't a couch any more, but merely a chair where you sat and talked to a trained counselor.

That was out.

Yet she needed somebody to talk to.

Finally the twenty blocks dragged to an end, and her mouth was still dry from the effort of walking through the late afternoon sun. The day had been warm and the heavy hot air of Southern California was still uncomfortably thick. A sign on the opposite side of the street announced *Hanson Trucking.* Jean went across the street to the large building.

Stepping into the small outer office she moved to the long counter and looked across at the attractive young redheaded woman who was sitting at a desk, typing. The woman was wearing a tight fitting white dress that clung sensually to her body: this was the kind of woman that a boss would consider quite a temptation.

Jean couldn't help wondering if this was the reason for Mary's jealousy.

"Is Joe Hanson in?" Jean asked.

"What is it you wished to see him about?" the woman inquired, impersonally, bringing her large eyes up to meet Jean's.

A sudden feeling shoved through Jean as she examined the woman's face. She was quite beautiful, very much like Debra Channings.

"I'm his sister-in-law."

"Oh, I'm sorry. Miss MacManners, isn't it?" The woman quickly stood and smiled. "I'll get him. He'll be surprised to see you here." The girl hesitated and then asked, "Is Mary—Mrs. Hanson here too?"

"No—I came alone." Jean hadn't missed the slight edginess to the other's voice as she had mentioned Mary.

The girl disappeared, and after a few minutes Joe Hanson came from the back room. "Well, will the world ever stop bringing surprises?" He seemed happy to see her. His brute features took on a strange, warm attractiveness as he looked into her eyes.

"I—could I talk to you?" Jean's voice faltered and then she leaned over the counter, closer to the man. She became aware of the animal smell of him and was surprised by the sharp effect it had on her nerves. "I left my money home—I wonder, could you loan me some?"

Joe looked puzzled. "Sure—but what's the bit?"

"Rather not talk about it. Had a little argument with Mary—nothing much—just that we got to talking about—about myself, and things got a little out of hand. I—well, to be truthful, this is all so silly, really...but I wanted...a drink and—*I feel like a damned fool!*" Jean lowered her eyes, suddenly aware of how silly she sounded.

Joe didn't show any reaction. "Forget it. People have their quibbles. Tell you what—I'll take a break and—we can have a drink together. I could use one."

"I thought you had to work late."

"I do—but I could use the break. There's nothing that says the owner and boss can't have a break with his attractive sister-in-law." He smiled warmly, patting Jean's arm.

She tensed under the touch, but smiled back. Suddenly she realized it had been a mistake to come to Joe.

She waited nervously for Joe to go to his office and return. He paused beside his secretary.

"If anybody wants me, Julie, we'll be at *Henry's*." He stepped around the counter and took Jean's arm. "Well, let's take off! I've been wanting to have a little private talk with you, and this'll give me a chance."

Jean's mind felt a spinning sensation. She followed the man out of the building to his car. They didn't say anything until he had brought the car to a stop several blocks away, in front of a cocktail lounge.

"I hope nothing happened you can't repair." Joe commented as he helped her. It was a moment before Jean could think of any way to sidestep a direct answer to his question.

"Sisters always have little fusses now and then. You gotta get used to it."

"I know—have a couple and they fought all the time. They live in San Francisco, and are now the best of friends." Joe explained as they walked into the dimly lighted cocktail lounge. He led Jean to a dark corner booth that was farthest away from the two other customers. Neither said anything until they had ordered two double martinis. Joe broke the silence.

"I guess you know there's some—tension is the best word—between Mary and myself."

Jean merely nodded. A sick feeling was beginning to gnaw at her.

"I don't know how to say it—it's just that well, maybe you could talk to Mary."

Jean wanted to scream.

"I don't really know you, Jean—but I feel I do because Mary told me a lot about you. You can learn quite a bit about a person that way. One thing I believe I *do* know for certain about you is that you've been around—not covered up and hidden away like Mary was. You've seen life pretty much the way it is." He hesitated and then continued. "What I'm really trying to say is—"

"Joe—I think I know what you're trying to say. Mary isn't much of a—to put it politely—a good wife in the bedroom."

Joe Hanson's features went silently grim and then seemed to crumble. The lost, hopeless expression in his eyes caused Jean to instinctively reach out a tender hand and touch his arm.

His fist slammed on the small table. "It's so damned maddening! To love somebody and have it be like this!"

"Joe—something like that can be caused by a lot of things," Jean offered gently.

The drinks came, and they were silent for a long time. Jean sipped the martini and felt the relief of

85

the cooling, smooth liquor sliding down her throat.

"We've tried everything," Joe explained in a whisper, as if talking aloud to himself.

"Maybe Mary expected too much—maybe it'll just take time," Jean suggested, taking another swallow of her cocktail.

"How much time?" Joe demanded. "If there hadn't been—well, if I'd been just a kid when I got married—I'd think it was my fault."

"Give her time."

"Could you talk to her?" Joe pleaded, looking desperately into Jean's eyes.

"I don't know. I don't think it'll do any good."

"Can you try?"

"I can try, but—I'll do my best. But what can I tell her?"

"Well, you've been around. Damn it all! I've told you this much—maybe I could tell you the rest!" He hesitated and then decided. "She just lays there. Doesn't do a damned thing! Just lays there and waits for me to get finished. If it weren't that I'm at the end of the line—about to burst—I wouldn't ask you—or anybody, to help!"

For some reason that seemed to end the conversation it had pushed too far, and both of them seemed to realize this.

When Joe finished his drink he pulled out his wallet and said, "I gotta go. You still want to borrow some money?"

"If you can spare it."

"How much?"

Jean was silent, thinking, and then said, "Maybe a twenty?"

He looked questioningly at her, but pulled out

two twenties, then a third one.

"I might not come home this evening, Joe," she told him. The alarm on his face caused her to quickly add, "Nothing *that* serious! Just that I need to be alone. Don't tell Mary you saw me...no, you better tell her something. Say I called you and said I wouldn't be back tonight. I have to think some things out, in private. You don't mind?"

"It's your life," Joe commented, standing. "I'll take care of the drinks. Thanks for letting me talk to you."

"Thanks for the drink."

The exchange had been surprising and totally different from what she had expected. He hadn't so much as even implied a pass; he was too involved with his own issues. He hadn't even really made much of her issues. Of course, she hadn't really opened up to him. Her reaction to it all was confused, empty and somewhat disappointed. But she did have the money.

Jean sat alone for a long time. When she had finished her first cocktail she stood and moved to the bar, sitting there on one of the stools. She hadn't consciously decided to get picked up, but there was an element in her mind that couldn't help playing with the idea. She wanted complete escape and had decided to let things work out. If some guy turned up and seemed interesting enough, who knew what she might do?

Her third martini started to daze her brain and, under the effect, she was leaning over the bar, conversing with the bartender. The conversation was general, at first, and then she asked, "Is there someplace where a girl can have a little fun?"

"What kind of fun are ya lookin' for?" the man inquired.

"The usual kind, I guess."

He studied her, then shrugged. "Around eight-thirty or so, things pick up here. You never can tell what might happen. A girl like you won't have any problem getting men's attention!"

She didn't like the implication, but realized it was exactly what she had been asking. For a long time she sat, confused, wondering why she was considering the prospect of getting picked up. Then, abruptly, Jean realized it was the last thing she really wanted. "Is there a liquor store about—and a place—a motel?"

The man stared at her. "You're sure a brazen one!"

"That's not what I meant!" Jean snapped, dropping her eyes. "I just wanted to go someplace to get quietly drunk. I changed my mind!"

She paid her bill without another word and left the bar. A man followed, tapping her on the shoulder.

"You want company?" he offered, grinning.

Jean turned and glared at him. He was around twenty-eight, and probably a college student—or a bum. "Go to hell!"

She jerked away and moved swiftly down the street. In a few moments she discovered a liquor store, walked in and bought a bottle of whiskey. She asked where there was a motel and got directions to one just a few blocks away. Half an hour later she was in a small motel unit, lying naked on the bed with a water glass full of whiskey.

It had been a long time since she'd done such a

thing—before going to New York. Getting slightly high, even a little "drunk" alone, sometimes made it possible for her to think a little more clearly. And Jean felt there was a lot of thinking to be done, a lot of mental sorting necessary. In that half-dazed state of semi-drunkenness her mind had an unusual clarity. She could think about the same things that bothered her while sober, without any emotional pain or hurt.

"You're a damned jerk!" Jean scolded herself, taking another swallow of whiskey. The liquor burned her throat, but went down smoothly. "And you're a little tramp, to boot. A whore, Lesbian tramp!"

Suddenly she wished that Debra were there to caress her with gentle, delicate fingers, to whisper in her ear that everything was all right, to run soft hands longingly down her body until she pleaded for release.

No! her mind screamed, *not that.*

Frank, and his concert of love, and his hands, rough and mannish, hard and coarse, so gentle and skilled, had literally seduced her. His lips clamping to her breasts, his tongue worrying the rigid and excited nipples were so thrilling. That's what she wanted; needed!

Why hadn't she waited and found out where he lived, what his phone number was? Joe would have told her. That had been a mistake. Then Jean forced herself to face the fact that it was probably better for her to be alone this evening, not to have the demand on her body to respond, when she was afraid that it might *not* respond. She needed this moment of time to think things out.

Another large swallow of whiskey settled into her stomach. She felt her body beginning to finally relax, to slowly slip away from her conscious ability to move.

This was the feeling she was waiting for, the desired effect.

In a little while the liquor would begin to relax her mind too, and sleep would drift over all awareness.

And then the dreaming?

No dreams! she told herself firmly. *No dreams, tonight!*

Another swallow of whiskey and she put the glass on the nightstand next to the bed and then slipped down under the covers, embracing the idea of complete, exhausted sleep.

It was some time before her mind began to float in that dark, dimensionless world of no time and no reality, that fantasy place where anything could happen, where anything was possible.

When sleep turned to dreams it was impossible for Jean to really know. There seemed no fine dividing line between reality and fantasy.

First there was darkness, a drifting sensation, a relaxing. Then her thoughts seemed to float without shape and without any real focus.

Visions of Debra and Frank formed for short moments and faded away. Then there was that horror world of breasts, but this time it quickly failed and in its place stepped the young redheaded woman that had been in Joe Hanson's office. Lovely and naked, inviting.

Jean heard her own voice cry out: "Oh. You're so lovely, dear." The woman grinned. Moistening

*her lips with the tip of her tongue. "I thought that
you might be one of us. A girl can tell."*

*Jean saw misty hands reach out and felt them
clasp over her breasts; the fingers worked longingly
on her nipples, making them become rigid and erect
with burning want. "Come on—let's go into my
bedroom," the woman invited. "There we'll discover the chambers of love within each of us…"*

*Jean was suddenly lying on a strange bed and
Joe Hanson was leaning over her. She knew he was
naked but couldn't make out the details of his body.*

*"Oh, honey, I've been wanting you ever since
you came here." His hands reached out and ran
lightly over her body.*

*Then Frank's voice exploded from the darkness.
"You told me I could have her!"*

*The hate and anger that flared in his voice
caused Jean to turn her eyes to the other side of the
bed. Frank was leaning over her, his hands reached
out and cupped over her breasts, as if guarding
them, protecting them. "She's mine!"*

"Men, such disgusting bastards!"

*Her heart pounded wildly at the sound of Debra.
Her eyes turned toward the door opening into the
strange bedroom in which she now was lying.
Standing there in black garters and bra, long black
gloves that went up to her elbows, and with a long
snake-like black whip clutched in her slender hands,
was Debra Channings. She had on her face the most
evil and horrifyingly sadistic expression Jean had
ever seen.*

*"She's mine, by right of conquest!" Debra
cried.*

The whip cracked out at Frank's hands, twice,

snapping once on each wrist, ripping the flesh into a broken bloody mass. "Lay your hands off my *woman!"*

The whip flashed out again, this time at Joe. "You horrible, sinful, degenerate man! You have a woman of your own. Go to her!"

Joe's chest opened with the terrible wound the whip made. He cringed back, clutching his chest, but the blood kept rivering out through his fingers.

Frank rushed forward, but was stopped short by the lashing whip's point, which cut at his groin.

Jean watched in horror as he doubled over in his agony, screaming.

"That's the sin of man! The sin that makes him defile woman! Defile the purity and virginity of women!" Debra shouted, flashing the whip from one cowering man to the other, until they were whimpering bulks of flesh, shivering and cringing at the terrible blows of that lightning, flashing whip point. Then the two men suddenly began to shrivel, dwindling in size, shrinking to the floor, becoming boneless blobs of trembling flesh and blood, screaming in agony, blending together into a pool of red liquid until they disappeared into the wooden floor.

Debra threw her whip aside and rushed to the bed.

"Oh, darling, why'd you leave me? Why couldn't you have stayed in New York? We could have been so happy together, so wonderfully happy." The longing expression on the woman face changed to sensual desire. Slowly, Debra removed her black bra, then the gloves, and, at last, the rest of the skimpy clothing, so that her body was bared

to Jean's hungry gaze.

"You *could have had all this! But you had to run away into the arms of another—into the arms of those men—those beasts and brutes. And for that you can never have me again!" Suddenly there appeared in Debra's hands a small pistol. "So, now you die! Die, for the traitor that you are!" the gun burst into flame.*

Jean caught the first bullet with her hand and it bounced off and then the second bullet dug deep into her stomach and she saw the little red hole it made. The third smashed at her chest, exploding there, bursting her breasts away. Another bullet shot down her screaming throat, like hot fire.

"Please, Debbie! I'll never leave you! I'll stay with you!" she pleaded as the blood started flowing from her body like a pulsing river.

"It's too late! The deed is done—finished. It is too late. All is too late!"

The voice kept repeating itself, kept saying over and over again that it was too late, even as the light of the morning sun broke through the motel window and crossed Jean's eyes, even as she sat up in the bed, her eyes opening and her head throbbing from a torturing headache.

"It's too late," her own voice was sobbing over and over. "It's too late!"

It was several minutes before Jean realized she was speaking the words. Then nausea flooded over her and her body suddenly became a convulsive sea of agony. She leaped from the bed and rushed to the bathroom, just making it in time.

Chapter Six

Frank stepped out of the shower, dried himself, and then, after putting on his shorts, stepped into the bedroom and over to the phone on the nightstand. The afternoon before, he had tried to get hold of Jean, but she was out. Mary Hanson had sounded as if she didn't know when to expect her in. Frank dialed and waited.

Joe Hanson answered.

"Is Jean there?" Frank asked.

"I'll go get her."

There was a long pause and then Jean's voice sounded meekly over the receiver.

"Hello?"

"Frank," he announced.

"I know, Joe told me."

"How're things?"

"Fine." But it sounded as if she was lying. Covering up. Her voice was guarded.

"Called to say how much I enjoyed the date."

"Thanks."

The flat, disinterested sound of her words startled Frank; but after a short hesitation he decided it probably had nothing to do with him.

"Wanted to know about the weekend. Can you make it? There's a nice place at Big Bear Lake I think you might enjoy. It should be heavy with snow, and if you like skiing there would be a—"

"I don't know. I *do* like skiing. Just that…"

"Then you'll come?"

There was hesitation again and he heard heavy breathing.

Finally she said, "Okay—why not? It'd be good to get the hell—well, get away a little while."

"Stay for the weekend?"

"Why not?"

"Okay—I'll pick you up tomorrow night about seven. That'll give me time to change, shower, and get to your place. We'll eat on the way."

"All right. That'll be fine." She paused and then quickly added, "Thanks for asking me."

"Think nothing of it. The pleasure's mine." He laughed.

A little while later Frank slowly hung up the phone. He stood there for a few moments and then went to his dresser, picked out a shirt and started getting dressed.

The evening with Jean had been one of the most satisfying times he'd had for a long while. There was something about the woman that pleased him. Maybe it was a forwardness, but not brazen like Kay Clifford.

Well, he thought happily, *Kay this evening, and Jean for the weekend.*

He felt pretty good.

Strangely, the idea of spending the night with Kay didn't overwhelmingly excite Frank. It was more a matter of not being alone. He would much rather have been with Jean. She was his new obsession of sorts; a nice, lovely and interesting female:

something of a puzzle and mystery. She seemed to be overly guarded. What could she be hiding? Obviously her life hadn't been perfect. Nobody's was. Maybe a bad love affair. In any case, he looked forward to breaking through that soft, yet solid wall that surrounded her, and getting to know the woman hiding there.

Kay was simply a nice habit that had filled many lonely nights. Before he left the apartment he had to fix himself a couple of weak highballs in order to get into the right mood for Kay. The woman could be sexually exhausting.

They had a long dinner at one of the Hollywood flash-atmosphere restaurants. He was distracted from the light conversation, reacting automatically while his mind kept being teased by thoughts of the coming weekend with Jean. The woman's image kept forming in his mind and there were times when he hardly heard Kay's voice. The drinks finally helped to refocus his attention on the woman. She was wearing a low cut evening dress that was brazenly revealing. He tired to focus on that. He had always enjoyed smothering himself against her lovely breasts. And the sight of them so openly displayed created an automatic animal response. By the time they returned to Kay's apartment, he was half loaded.

When the door closed, Frank buried himself in the fullness of Kay's lips, taking in the softness of her mouth, his hands tightly gripping her.

She strained to him.

"Oh, Frank, you're so *hard!*" she laughed, hands reaching between them for a moment. "And I'm so hot!"

He gripped her by the hips and pulled her up off the floor. It was an automatic action, and even while reacting to the woman's body, mentally he was wondering what it would be like to do these very things with Jean. The image of that woman was almost a three-dimensional reality in his mind. In fact, he found his thoughts surrounding her mental image, making love to her with his lips, hands.

Kay sobbed, clutching her arms about his neck, swinging her legs about his hips for support. He hadn't even been aware of her having opened his pants, and was hardly surprised to discover she wasn't wearing any panties. That was Kay, ready for instant. It was quick and dirty and when they had both climaxed, she sobbed out a low, savage moan, then fell to her knees before him. For Kay the evening of lovemaking had only begun, not ended. And she now went fairly wild.

He found his own sexual energies driven beyond control by her. Yet during all of it, there was only a thin thread of his mind paying any attention to what was going. He was thinking only of Jean.

He responded to her carnal actions and she moaned in delight.

Mentally he had been making love to Jean, and not to the convulsively clawing and wiggling Kay Clifford. He started returning the caresses and finally the kisses, but with a tenderness that was totally focused on another woman's image. The feelings welled up through him, commanding every caress, every kiss into a new, intensely fired level of giving, not taking, of wanting to literally overwhelm the woman with worshipping love.

Oh, how I love you, Jean, his mind murmured

softly to the phantom image in his head. It didn't even seem strange to think such a thing as long as he never really meant it. Fantasy love was one thing. Yet, the intense sense of emotion behind that thought was stunning. It was almost as if he really meant it; as if he were mentally enveloping Jean's very soul. The whole experience was numbing and even confusing. For a few moments it seemed as if Jean was in his arms at that very instant. Only with conscious will was he able to avoid saying her name. He tried to center his mind on Kay, to remember it was this lovely, nice lady who so totally captured him. He knew Kay; didn't know Jean. They had been intimate for a long time; and had been very close in so many ways. Yet the image of Jean kept surging back into his mind again and again.

He smothered himself against Jean/Kay, discovering the woman's full breasts, kissing them with tenderness he had never expressed before with any woman. This was a lovely, goddess, and a creature of heaven, who had descended down to him like an overwhelming blanket of loving perfection. And when he entered her, as she literally surrounded his whole being. His mind was focused on Jean. And it seemed that she was with him, responding to his very soul as it blended so anxiously with her fantasy image It was total illusion, and even while a part of him was annoyingly aware of whose body he was so deeply penetrating, his mind kept clawing desperately at the delicious, wonderful thought of Jean.

The woman had become an obsession he couldn't escape! And he made love to her though Kay's body.

Afterwards, Kay clung to him, happily kissing his lips and cheeks and neck.

"You are wonderful, Frankie, oh, so wonderful! I never knew you could be like that. So wonderful. I do love you. I love you so very, very much, Frankie. And I know you love me—you couldn't make love like that if you didn't. Oh, you are wonderful! So, so desperately wonderful!" She bubbled on and on, telling him how much she had needed and loved him from the moment he had first taken her body and shown her what it was like to be really loved; told him how much it meant to her that he really *did* care, now that his love-making had revealed his true feelings toward her.

But Frank hardly heard the words; his mind didn't even catch their meaning. He was thinking about other things, other moments, and the prospect of the next days. He was thinking about Jean MacManners.

Later, he sat up in bed and slid his legs over the side.

"Where're you going?" Kay demanded, startled.

"I have a long day tomorrow."

"Well, so do *I!*" she exclaimed, miffed.

"All the more reason to leave."

For a moment Kay didn't say anything, she just sat on the bed, apparently numbed by his sudden change of attitude. He was distant, faraway, as if he weren't even aware of her lying there near him, naked, as if he hadn't even heard her words.

"You must be kidding!"

Frank turned and patted Kay's cheek, realizing that he was probably hurting her very deeply. He didn't want to hurt her.

"Don't be ridiculous! You can't expect to have breakfast with me every time. I really should be going."

He forced himself to lean down and kiss her gently on the lips. He did care about her as a human being; and in his way probably loved her as a person but not as a lover.

Her hands clawed at his head, holding it down, not wanting to release him.

Carefully, he pushed away, moving her hands from his neck. Then seeing the hurt expression on her face, he said, "If I take that kind of punishment long I won't be leaving!"

It was intended to be a gentle kind lie.

"Then why leave?" Kay demanded, pouting.

"It's late, past two. If I don't get home I'll not get any sleep!"

His mind pleaded with Kay to keep quiet, to not question him any further. For her own sake. He didn't want to hurt her.

This evening had proven one thing completely to Frank: the affair with Kay Clifford was finished, it only had to be gently brought to an end, without hurting her; it wasn't really Kay's fault.

He didn't want anybody except Jean MacManners to have his attentions; why he felt that way Frank didn't want to even question, let alone attempt to understand—it terrified him because of its unexpected presence. He was afraid to understand, because of what it might reveal. Frank didn't want to know that much about the way he thought or desired.

Live from day to day and take what is desired and offered—but don't ask "Why?" because the an-

100

swer might scare you off and there wouldn't be any of the pleasure which mere blind taking could offer.

This had been his unconscious motto for years. He invoked it fully now, refusing to think about the motives which controlled him.

Getting quickly dressed, Frank threw a kiss to Kay and after telling her how good it had been and how much he had enjoyed himself, he quietly left.

Once in the car, he realized what a bore the evening had really turned out to be. Oh, there had been a few moments, he admitted reluctantly, but nothing to compare to those he had shared with Jean the other night. There was something about Jean that had captured his imagination; and made him want to be protective to her. They were feelings he hadn't felt for years—not since that time he had gotten his first crush on a college girl and then thought that he was finally in love. His first real *love* affair.

Tonight he had made love to Kay merely because it was expected.

On the way home, Frank was worried about what he'd learned about himself this evening; wondered how he had been so completely captured by the need for a woman he'd only met twice.

He puzzled all night, tossing on the bed, not finding rest until early morning.

* * * * * * *

Joe Hanson looked down at his wife, who had just slipped under the bed covers. She was, to him, an angel of purity, a lovely beauty who had drawn him into a web of emotions to which he felt eternally bound; a statue of simple beauty that had no inner fire, made of cold stone; and, stone-like, was merely an outer shell without inner erotic, passionate feelings.

Strangely, after a year of marriage, he couldn't think of her as anything else. At least, when it came to emotions of the flesh. She felt nothing sexually except the desire to be held gently, told how much he loved her, but without any inner need to be caressed and kissed. She wanted a spiritual love, which he had willingly given her, because he felt that way about her; but he wanted to give more and wanted to receive more, like any normal person.

"What in the world are you doing?" Mary demanded, opening her eyes and looking up at him. Then, as she saw the expression on his face, a hardness and a helpless acceptance clouded her eyes. "Oh, that! Don't you think about anything else?"

For a moment Joe had the impulse to yell at her, shout that this wasn't the *only* thing that he thought about, but was the one thing he wanted in order to complete their marriage into a perfect whole. Instead, he stepped to the bed and sat down next to his wife.

"Mary—why do you have to be like that?"

"Like what?" her voice demanded stiffly, defensively.

"You know there's nothing wrong with what I want and need."

"And I guess there's something wrong in the way I feel about it?" The words were only words, exploded on the silence of the dimly lit room: they held no muscle of conviction because she knew it was her fault; and that she was the one who was wrong; perhaps even flawed.

102

"There's nothing wrong with you, Mary, just that you're maybe a little afraid of your emotions." He reached out and caressed her cheek the way he knew she liked him to do.

"I'm sorry. I do love you so much, Joe—but I don't know…I want you to hold me and I want you to make love to me…but I just can't help it…feeling what I feel, or not feeling what you want me to. I'm me. I told you…just accept what I can give…and things will be okay. I'm what I am…you say you love me…but you don't accept how I am. You can have me…sure…you know that…only…I can't promise something I'm…not!"

Joe's lips covered hers and she mechanically responded. He knew she was only doing what he expected her to do. It was a bland, non-passionate act.

Open offering given on the Altar of Marriage: *because this was her duty.*

How he hated that!

Yet many marriages survived in such a static state; events, life itself just simply got in the way of a couple's sex life. And then, also, the getting so used to one another that boredom sets in.

Mary had never been very passionate, even in the beginning. And the more they had sex the more distant she became, as if each experience simply proved to her how hopeless it was, how little she cared about it.

Was she normal? Or was she frigid?

Or was he simply obsessed with sex?

Was there something wrong with him wanting a passionate wife who would seek pleasure in his arms?

No, damn it! Joe silently admitted to himself,

fighting down the anger that threatened to well up like an explosion.

But there it was. She lacked the passion. He was driven mad with it. The less she wanted the more he desperately needed.

Suddenly the desire, the longing and the demand of wanting her moved through his mind; he hadn't touched Mary for weeks and now he didn't care any more what she wanted or what she didn't want.

He had needs and damn it all, he would at least take what little was being offered. As he always, finally, did.

It was his right to take her, and she knew it, and she was willing to give herself to him.

They kissed. Mary lay there passively, not really responding to his kisses. Joe's hands moved over her body with the skill of a trained lover. She just let him touch and caress her, but was like a stone statue.

His hands had known the bodies of many women. In Japan they had loved, and in Mexico they had loved, and in California, Idaho, Arizona, and Georgia they had loved and known the responses of hungry, passionate women. Those others had moved wildly, they had clawed at him, they had cried for more caresses and more hungry kisses; they had moaned and sighed and they had cursed against the pain and pleasure.

Sure, some might have been doing the ol' fake job. But not all of them! And at least those who did fake it offered an illusion: a feeling of mutually charged union. The illusion was better than having, for all intents and purposes, almost a dead body letting itself be used in the act of "doing her wifely duty!"

Mary lay there, submitting herself to his touches, lovemaking, but not giving *of* herself. There were no "counterpunches" nothing to really inspire passion even in him. Yet his own mental passion mixed with the normal animal needs of his body was enough to keep him driving at her with furious abandon.

Angrily, almost brutally, Joe clasped her breasts between his hands and moved his lips downwards until they were smothered in the silken softness of them, smothered in their full supple loveliness.

"You're hunting," was Mary's only remark, her only reaction.

For a moment Joe froze, numbed by the coldness of her remark, infuriated by the lack of emotion, the hard bitterness that it held. The first impulse was to move away, leave the house and go where he could pick up some tramp. That would give him the release his body really needed; yet not with the woman he wanted. There had been enough of sluts and barroom tramps in his life to end all desire for such shallow relations. But wasn't their sex life horridly shallow in a totally different way?

Suddenly the emotion exploded up through him, fury that had been bubbling for months, since the first night of his honeymoon when he'd discovered that Mary was so sexually cold.

"You goddamned bitch!" he cursed under his breath. "Not this time! Not *this* time!" His lips closed around a soft nipple. His hands clawed brutally, savagely.

"Joe," Mary gasped, struggling.

But he ignored her. This time he was going to

take her any way it was possible: even if brutal force was necessary. Screw her icy comments designed to shut him down. Fuck her!

His hands worked over her body, finding the hidden zones that he most desired to touch, stripping the covers from her and covering her body with kisses. She fought wildly and he was forced to hold her hands down at her sides with his knees. Horror clouded her face but she was helpless under his brute strength. Then, in a way he'd never done with a woman before, he started roughly caressing and kissing her breasts, working them as if hoping that in this brutal way desire could be forced into her body; hoping that she would magically come to life.

"Let me alone—please—I'll call Jean—I'll call my sister!" she hissed in desperation, starting to open her mouth as if to scream.

Joe clamped his hand over her lips.

"Fuck you. Shut up! Be quiet!" he hissed in such a threatening voice that her eyes revealed the fear his words had put into her.

He rammed himself against her, letting her feel the hardness of his erection against her.

Let her know how much he hurt wanting her!

Then a sudden change took place in Mary Hanson; a strange and unexpected change. His caressing seemed to be tightening her muscles. The rosy centers of her breasts began to stiffen and for the first time he saw her eyes half close in pleasure. A low, hardly audible moan sounding from her now parted lips.

Joe didn't stop to think or to understand, he just continued his caressing, letting his hands find the zones that caused little trembles to move through

106

her body. Then, when he instinctively knew it was the right moment, he released her arms and they slipped hungrily around his back, drawing him down to her. In the next few moments their bodies blended into one, until the rhythm had finally strained them together for the last time, and then they fell exhausted in that half-sleep aftermath of ecstasy, both totally stunned by what had just happened.

* * * * * * *

And in the other bedroom Jean, even in her sleep, tossed in anguish. Her face tensed, a moan sounded from her parted lips and her body writhed sensually. She frowned and then her teeth clamped down hard on her lips, turning them white under the pressure.

The dream passed and she relaxed and for a long time rested, her breathing becoming normal in natural sleep. Then, early in the morning, as the world of breasts burst into existence before her sleep-mind, she shivered and tensed again.

"Those men—kill those ugly little men!" her *mouth whispered. Her hands reached up to her breasts, slapping at them. "That's better!"*

Then she went tense again.

"Get off—you little beasts—get off!" she cursed softly. Her lips smiled happily. "Oh, Debbie! Debbie! Thank God! Yes—" Then her words were mere sounds of desire, pleasure, longing.

Her body stiffened and she writhed under the covers. Then her lips snarled: "Frank.... No!! I want Debbie!"

107

Expressions struggled over her features, from confusion to hate, from love to desire, from desire to anger and puzzlement.

"I don't love you, Frank! You know that! I don't love you!"

She went rigid, tense. She twisted on the bed and then tensed once more. "Yes, yes. Yes, I do love you. I do love you, Frank! I don't care about anything else. Just you!"

She hesitated and then said, "Go away, Debbie. I don't want you."

The covers moved from her naked body.

"No!" she shouted, sitting up in bed.

"No!" she whispered, trembling.

For a moment she sat there, her eyes wide open, breathing hard, dazed and not sure where she was. Then a convulsion of horror rippled down her body and she closed her eyes against the pain of the dream that had wakened her.

It was a long time before she found rest again and this time no dreams came. Ste didn't awaken until late in the morning.

Chapter Seven

Sitting in the car next to Frank as they drove up the mountain road, Jean was thinking about her sister, Mary. Ever since she had told Mary about the "Woman in New York," things had been terribly stilted. But this morning and afternoon, Mary had been strangely detached, faraway; she'd been slightly brooding. She had sat looking off into space, a dazed and frightened expression on her face. Jean had been worried and tried to find out what was wrong, but Mary refused to talk about it. Joe hadn't returned home by the time Frank picked Jean up.

"Jean?" Frank's voice cut into her thoughts.

"Yes?"

"I've been thinking about you."

She didn't know what to say to that so she remained silent.

"I've never met a girl like you, Jean. You have the damnedest effect over me."

"Should I thank you for that?" she inquired, smiling.

"I believe so. That was the way I meant it."

They were silent for a long time, but Jean's thoughts now centered on Frank and what he had said and what if anything she felt for him.

He's a nice man, she realized. *After the brazen way she'd acted the other evening, he might have felt differently about her. But he treated her with respect. That was nice. Considering.*

Jean blushed and her eyes turned to the surrounding darkness that blanketed the car. The night was blackness pinpointed by the subtle brightness of the Milky Way and all its diamond children.

"It's a beautiful night, isn't it?" she offered thoughtfully.

"Wait 'till you get to the lake."

"I've been there before but I was awfully young, so I hardly remember!"

"You'll remember this time. I checked on the weather and they say it should snow tonight or tomorrow. The roads are clear as of now, but they should be covered—at least momentarily—by tomorrow afternoon."

"Be able to get some skiing in?"

"There's snow on the hills now, so I'm told, so I guess things'll be pretty good."

"Where're we staying?"

"At the *Winter Lodge*. Run by Karl Winter. Spelled 'Winter,' pronounced 'Vinter'—German."

"That's quite a proper name, considering," Jean laughed.

"Been in the States for over twenty years. Remembers the early years of Hitler and well, he has quite a lot of interesting stories to tell. Each night he'll sit in front of the huge fireplace—in the lobby—and filling his pipe thoughtfully, coughing a couple of times, and then lighting his pipe, he'll sit there reflecting for several minutes and then begin to tell stories dating back almost seventy years. He's an old man, but you'd never know he's almost eighty. Hell of a nice guy!"

They drove for a long time without saying anything and it wasn't until they came to the *Winter Lodge* that the conversation picked up. A little later Jean was unpacking her things in the small, three-room cabin Frank had rented. It had a miniscule bedroom, a little front room, and a tiny kitchen. The walls were off gray and there was a heater in the center of the living room. Frank was off getting ice for cocktails.

After unpacking, Jean sat in the living room before the heater, enjoying the cozy atmosphere. Outside, snow was lightly sprinkled over the land. The air was chilly and there was a slight breeze. She hoped it was true that there was supposed to be snow during the night.

Frank returned in a flurry of coldness. He was carrying a paper ice bucket filled to the brim.

"You sure we needed it?" Jean laughed.

"How's that?" Frank shivered and moved to the heater, standing very near Jean.

"Ice. We could have passed the glasses outside for a moment. That would have chilled them."

"Maybe you have a point! It's really getting cold. Feels like a thousand below zero." He stood there for a moment and then stepped into the kitchen. After a couple of minutes he returned with two highballs. "Well, here's to you."

Jean took the glass he offered and sipped from it. The drink was strong.

She felt damned good. It was fun being with Frank. She had almost been afraid—before he picked her up—but now, in his presence, she felt

111

relaxed and comfortable.

"What's on for tomorrow?" she inquired, happily.

"Oh, maybe a little skiing like we planned—and a little singing in the evening with the group at the Lodge. I'd like you to meet Karl and hear some of his stories. Then, there's the lake, a lot of scenery and things like that."

"Sounds fun. I'm glad you asked me up here."

"I'm glad you came!" Frank exclaimed, honestly.

"Now that the formalities are over," Jean giggled gaily, "what's next?"

Frank leaned closer to her and touched her cheek with his lips. "Is that good for a starter?"

Jean held back the inner tension and smiled. "Why not?"

They didn't say anything more while finishing their drinks and then, after he had refilled them, they sat and talked about themselves. Frank told her something about his past. He had grown up on a farm and lived pretty much of a country life until getting into the service during the Korean War, then afterwards had gone through college, with the help of the G.I. Bill.

"Those were rough times but they had their fun."

"Women?" Jean teased. She felt suddenly light headed and realized that the mixture of clear mountain air and liquor had made her somewhat high much sooner than it would have in Los Angeles.

"There were some girls," he admitted, briefly.

"Anything serious?"

"I don't think it's nice to talk about other affairs

112

to a woman with whom you're being intimate."

"I guess you're right. I'm sorry, Frank. I was only teasing, really. Conversational fencing, I guess."

"Talking about conversation…how about some?" Frank inquired, serious faced, but eyes gleaming.

"Isn't that what we're doing?" Jean asked, puzzled, wondering where the gag was hiding.

"Conversation, according to some dictionaries I've known, is defined as the relations between man and woman…physically." His smile was broad and full, his eyes brightly laughing.

Jean felt herself blush. Her mind raced: *This man has a strange effect over you. Why should you be reacting like that? Why is it that you are excited by the idea of going to bed with him and yet terrified at the same time?*

There are more things in heaven and earth, dear little Jean, than you'll ever dream of or understand. Stop questioning. Try to just enjoy yourself!

Jean forced a laugh and quickly finished her drink. "Why not?"

After turning out the lights, they went into the bedroom. In the darkness, only broken slightly by the moonlight filtering like a pale golden haze through the window, Frank found her body; his hands gently drew her to him.

The nearness of his large form was like a soothing glove that fit so perfectly that Jean suddenly felt at home, at last, at the time and place she was meant to be. It was the mood and the room and the setting and the excitement of the trip, she reasoned. And getting away from her sister's home with all those conflicts that seethed under the surface. It was getting away with somebody new that made this so wonderful now. For this nice man was basically a stranger; but one whom she was getting to know better and to actually like.

That was the only logical explanation.

His hands whispered along her body, drawing aside her sweater and then her skirt until she was left with only bra and panties between herself and his body.

They remained standing, clutching against each other, their lips just touching. The hardness of his body was thrilling. She felt her breath becoming more strained in her lungs, her skin heated as if some solar flame had been bathed over it. It was comfortable being in Frank's arms; it was complete and nothing could be added to make it better; at least for the moment. Frank seemed to sense the mood, for he led her gently to the bed. They settled down, just lying close to one another.

This seemed a time for simply sharing silence and awareness of one another, without straining to do anything else. Just being together seemed enough.

They didn't move for a long time, then Frank gently slipped away into the darkness and returned with a pack of cigarettes. He lighted one and handed it to her and then lighted a second, taking a deep drag.

Jean's eyes looked out the window at the white glistening of the moon peeking through the trees surrounding their cabin.

"It's funny," Frank said in a thoughtful voice, "that sometimes it isn't right to defile a romantic mood by lowering it to mere passion."

Jean smiled and reached out to clasp his hand, intertwining her fingers affectionately with his.

The nearness of him excited her in a way she hadn't felt for a long time. Her mind wondered if this was the feeling women talked about when entering into a real love affair. There *was* a difference. Sometimes passion was wrong, and it would be a sin to break this mood for the physical desire of the body. Sometimes it was necessary to entertain the soul. Assuming they had one. That was a strange thought to her and suddenly she wanted to talk to Frank about it.

"You believe in God?"

"Which God?" he asked absently.

"A God with a gray beard and—"

"That idea went out with—well it went out a long time ago. At least for me." He paused, and then his voice was serious when he asked, "Why?"

"I don't know. I got to thinking about what you said—and how it is necessary to sometimes feed the soul. But I never was one to believe either way about a soul—or life after death, really. I sometimes wonder just what God is, and what—if anything—the soul is. An illusive foggy thing? Something invisible. Does it exist in a different dimension? Where…is it now?"

"The soul is that within you which is the spark of God or the spark of life. At least that's what I was told by somebody. I always believed there is a soul in man, but not necessarily in the way others think of it. The spark of life and love, it is that thing which responds to love and responds with love— that is the soul, I suppose. Call it Mind or call it God

115

or call it 'that *of* God'—or what you will, but it is that something which is—and I hate using the term—divine."

"Then—if there is that Divine—what does it think about us? And what we are doing?"

"You think that somebody that has had—No! Put it this way: do you believe that something which could have created all the stars, the sun and moon and all there is in the universe and all the galaxies in the sky, and all there is, would be interested in what *you*—Jean MacManners—and *me*—Frank Martin— do? As long as we don't hurt anybody or thing? I believe that we are put on this earth for the purpose of living. I believe—assuming that there *is* a God— and surely there must be something that caused all *this* to be—I believe that to love and to express love and kindness is the most important thing in the world to do. Marriage is man-made law. Marriage, to me, is in the mind alone. You are married by your inner feelings at the moment. Rigid, dogmatic, moral ethics are for the birds!"

"That's pretty far out, isn't it?" Jean asked, thoughtfully.

"Not really. Hell, you take these damned closed-minded prudes who go to church every Sunday. Sure, there are some that are good—but too many of them do mouth-service to their God, and on Monday lay other people's wives and husbands. Damn it all! To live a good life is to do what you believe to be right—as long as you aren't going out hurting others—and to give as much of yourself as you can to others. I'd rather never go to church, but live a good life, helping others and expressing a joy for life and for love, than just express the 'lip service' too many churchgoers do.

"There've been more wars and killing and pillage and rape caused by the wars fought in the name of God than for any other reason. And what God is *the* God? Either one—or all? I believe that what a man does and what a man believes is between himself and *his* God. There are as many religions in the world as there are people, because everybody understands ideas and words differently. No two people think alike. I've made my peace with the Maker. I do try to live a right and good life—and I go out of my way to add to the world around me and not just take.

"Sure, there have been women in my life but I've never gone out and consciously tried to seduce a virgin. Or demoralize those who believe certain ways. All I ask, in return, is that others leave me alone to live the kind of life I desire. I can't help believing that the reward comes in living by what you *honestly* believe in and doing your best to be true to those beliefs.

"As for what a Maker might think of what we are doing—that depends on what *we* think about it. Do we feel guilty? Do we feel it is wrong?"

"Then you're saying that Hitler was right because he *believed* he was right." Jean pointed out.

"No. Not at all. You can't forget my one point: *as long as what you do does no harm to others around you!*

"I told you that I believe you should express the living and creative and loving elements of your personality. Give of yourself. Not stupidly but expressing that within you which is worth expression. That's what I believe. Wrong or right. I'll die and receive my 'reward' or hell on those beliefs." Frank paused and then added, more lightly, "Hell, we might as well enjoy ourselves—for tomorrow we might be blown into tiny atoms by the all out war."

"A depressing thought."

"A depressing one, sure but none the less a real possible one!"

"Can't we talk about something less depressing?" Jean requested, feeling a little nervous about the sudden drift of the conversation. She had never been sure how she really felt about life and things like that, but knew there was "Something" which directed—and that "Something" was called, for lack of a better term, God.

Probably what bothered her, she reasoned, was that Frank had pretty much expressed her own vague ideas.

Jean was aware of his hand moving along her thigh, and the feeling it caused brought her mind back to the present. A shiver rushed through her. His hand came to rest against her panties.

"Do you think that was nice?" she laughed nervously, playfully pushing his hand away.

"Of course. What do you think? You're a maiden, and, as for myself, I'm a sex hungry knight, just back from saving the king's life, after twenty years of battle—without a woman, I might add—and I'm a little anxious to get on with the action. Can you blame me?"

Suddenly they weren't talking any more, or thinking about talking. They were straining together, frantically kissing, anxiously squirming tighter. In the next minutes Frank reached under her back and skillfully removed her bra and minutes

118

later he caressed off her panties. There wasn't any moment of awkward waiting, for he moved over her with hands and lips and body, flooding away all thought except the sensual pleasure of the moment.

The touch of his fingers ran over her thighs, then lingered, thrillingly.

Jean writhed, a low moan of pleasure uttering from her.

He slowly lifted her hips, then with expert skill, turned her around, stomach down on the bed.

She thrilled, wondering what new form of erotic pleasure might be offered.

His hands slipped under her chest and then his lips started lightly caressing one earlobe.

"Oh, Frank, what...are you doing!" she sobbed as his fingers lightly stroked her nipples.

"Loving you, Jean," he said softly, pulling her earlobe between moist lips, teasing it with the tip of his tongue.

God, she thought, *he's loving me like wild.*

"Oh, Frank," she sobbed, clutching at the pillow.

At that point his hands gripped her hips, tugging them upwards and she felt him suddenly penetrate her in one simple move.

That fast it happened; and she had been more than ready, anxious for him to enter her.

They both moved as one.

"Oh. Frank." she cried again, gasping for breath when he moved his hands up against the full swells of her breasts where they half hung in the air above the bed. She could hardly breathe when he lightly palmed them.

The next moments were a heavenly awareness

119

of him moving, but she could think of nothing other than the waves of lovely sensation that whip up through her whole body. It was electric and wonderful. She felt dizzily drunk with pleasure. She felt his hardened stomach muscles press the soft curves of her fanny and her fingers clawed at the pillow.

She was riding a sea of sensations, aware of nothing other than the thrilling bliss of her lover being one with her in every possible way. It was an ecstasy so wonderful that she could hardly hold on to her sanity. To Jean, it was like frantically flying into some unreal dimension beyond which there was little reality other than the endless waves of joyous, caressing pleasure that drown everything else in its wild intensity.

Frank suddenly turned Jean, until the bed pressed up against her back. With a deep sigh of contented pleasure, she anxiously wrapped her legs about him, clutching at him like a savage wild animal that has been totally impaled. Again they were locked together as one total being, complete, experiencing one another, experiencing the utter union of unlimited ecstasy. After what seemed an endless wave of pleasure, she fell back on the bed, exhausted. Sleep clouded over her mind and body.

Awareness of Frank covering her face and lips with gentle, love-kisses, brought her attention back to the present.

"You were wonderful...wonderful, Jean," he told her in a passionate voice.

She slipped her hands about his neck, covered his lips with. The taste of him was delicious. As the kiss broke, she smiled. "*You* were *fantastic*! It all happened so fast!"

"Yes...but the build up had been hellish! Days, years...a lifetime."

"That all?" she smiled, contentedly.

"No, really a rather long eternity. And it is only started...I want to love you forever."

"I thought...it was over...That was just wonderful what you did to me!"

They pressed together and she became aware of the fact that Frank was already beginning to respond to her nearness.

She didn't say anything, because her mind was bathed in the wonderful feel of this. She wanted him again.

"Frank, Frank!" she moaned, suddenly not caring about anything but the feel of the man, the hungry wanting of him to be in her again. She wanted to be aware of the oneness of their bodies united in loving wild tenderness, mad abandon passion.

And they made love, their hands, lips, and their whole bodies surging hungrily at one another, like they were starved and feasting on the banquet of their mutual love. For it was love of such power, and of such lovely sensations that she couldn't even think. This was something so pure and innocent, so utterly complete that nothing else existed nor mattered. They were moving through an endless sea of pleasure, mutually shared, without restraint.

"Frank!" she cried, driven beyond any kind of control. A part of her wanted to scream that she loved him. But of course the words didn't form. They would be insane. How could she love somebody she didn't even really know? This was mad passion; and she simply loved the way he totally possessed her in such a lovely, wonderfully skilled way. She choked on her own thoughts, mere animal moans sounded from her throat.

"Oh, Jean..."

Then she was mentally smashed against such ecstatic pleasure that consciousness slammed momentarily away.

In the morning things changed in a lovely way, becoming amazingly different.

It was almost impossible, upon waking next to Frank, to keep from offering herself. But somehow it didn't seem proper. There was a time and place for such wild abandon. She was almost frightened by how he'd turned her into such an animal, totally possessed, totally overwhelmed with a raw, uncontrolled need for him.

They embraced for a tender moment.

Then he'd said he was hungry for something to eat.

"You really drained me, last night!" he'd laughingly told her, winking playfully.

They had taken turns in the shower, though she'd been tempted to call him into the stall with her. It was difficult to keep from being a sexual cat-in-heat with Frank; but she wanted to be something more than just a little whorish weekend thrill! What that might be, she didn't even consider.

Instead, she had simply played it by ear, following his example; his manly lead.

So they got ready for breakfast at the lodge.

But all through breakfast her thoughts centered on their lovemaking. He had been so wonderful. She was deliciously overwhelmed by the experience of being with him. She loved gazing into his eyes, watching him move, eat.

The snow that had come in the night covered the mountains with its whiteness and Frank's suggestion that they ski had been an attractive one. They seemed more like lovers than merely sexual partners; they were involved in more than just the orgiastic side of one another; and she found this highly pleasing. He didn't just think of her as a good little lay. And that seemed important.

The air was chilled, though refreshing. On the ski lift, Jean felt as if she were in a world of her own, without any other soul around her, only the whiteness and the mountains and the green of the trees. Nature, naked and bare. It was a feeling she hadn't had for a long time and one that continued even when she joined Frank at the top of the mountain. He helped her with the skis and then they stood there at the top of the ski run, which stretched out far below them, the wind cold across their cheeks.

"You'll be on your own, Jean," Frank warned. "You sure you can handle it?"

"I *think* so!" she laughed. "It's a long way down."

"Race me?"

"No. But where do we meet?"

"The cocktail lounge?"

"That's an idea. Hot buttered rum after a long ski ride, that's a *good* idea."

They stood there for a little longer and then Jean suddenly pushed off, feeling the breeze make her cheeks pink.

The thrill of standing alone against the mountain, straining with her own personal power and skill against the slopes of fleecy white, caused her heart to beat wildly, her blood to race.

For a long time she didn't think about anything except her movement through the wind. Once it became instinctive again, since it had been some months since she'd been skiing, she remembered suddenly the last time, with Debra Channings, she had gone skiing. They had rented a cabin and stayed for a couple of weeks. It was the first time they'd been together for more than a night, and the excitement had been almost as deeply rewarding as it was now, with Frank. The only thing that had marred it was the fact it was an illicit affair, without the normality of male-female relationship. She hadn't gotten used to it, but thought that in time the guilt might truly disappear as Debra had promised her it would. But it never had. Not for her. Some people were quite comfortable with that life-style; and it was right for them. But she'd felt deeply disturbed by it, even when things had been beautiful.

The first evening had developed much as it had with Frank. They had had cocktails and then gone to bed. Debra had told her not to feel guilt, that there wasn't anything wrong with what they were doing. "*We* have a right to pleasure just like the others," she had explained. Then her hands had given Jean pleasure, moving over her with intimate skill, racing the desire up through all the levels of excitement until it had become ecstasy.

Memory of that evening and then the evenings later caused Jean's body to become excited and created a sudden gnawing longing for the woman. Then the image of Frank's hard, muscular, man's body blended over the feminine form, and Jean felt another need, another desire which was much the same, but strangely different. And welcomed.

How could a woman love two people, each of a different sex? she wondered, annoyed with herself.

Then the thought that she "loved" ran through her, waved like electric currents were being charged across her nerve endings.

Love Frank? That didn't seem possible! She hardly knew him. Yet, if love was the need of one person for another, to express itself and to be returned by the object of the desire, then she was in "love" with Frank.

That much Jean realized, even though she lacked understanding of it.

All that had flashed through her mind in a split second.

Then her thoughts centered on the light images in front of her eyes.

The trees were slashing past her, other skiers were moving at all sides of her.

Instinctively she came to a suddenly stop, trying to spot Frank, but it just wasn't possible. The snowy hill was speckled with little fleeing dots of color, and nobody could really recognize any one from another.

She stood there for some time, thinking, puzzled by her thoughts, frustrated by them.

What was love, anyway? And why did she care a damn about such things? she wondered, annoyed by such thoughts. *Was love nothing but the rationalization of the sex impulse?*

Then, little woman, you could be in love with anybody that you sexually desired!

But that was impossible, Jean realized.

Angrily, she tried once more to turn her thoughts away to other subjects.

Frank's image returned to her mind's eye.

Frank and his wonderfully caressing hands and lips.

It was a strange and puzzling thing to be loved by a woman and also by a man, and enjoy both.

It was also a little terrifying.

What was wrong with her, to make it possible to desire lovers of both sexes? Could she ignore one side of her personality and push it, shove it, if necessary, with force—down into a deep recess of her mind and forget it was ever there?

Once more she attempted to draw her mind away from the agonizing mental questioning.

Shaking her head, she started down the hill again. Her eyes were now focused on the world around her which was spinning hurriedly by.

She slid down into a hollow and then flew madly over a slight rise, momentarily floating in the air, and felt the jar of impact as she once more made contact with the fleecy white snow. She twisted around one tree and then around another. It was like escaping dark shadows against white. Like dancing among the trees in some heavenly place where humans simply did not exist.

For a long time Jean was able to forget her thoughts and worries and questions and enjoy the ride down the hill of white, until finally the lodge showed through the trees, far in the distance, and she began to wonder if Frank had already arrived and ordered drinks. She hoped so.

It was cold, and her bones felt as if ice had touched them with a frigid hand. A shiver rushed through her as she finally sliced past the last trees, slowing down in her approach to the large central

126

building where the restaurant and lodge were located.

Finally, after coming to a speedy stop, Jean stepped out of the skis and returned them to the rental stand, and, after clapping her hands on her flushed cheeks, she moved into the lodge and entered the cocktail lounge.

The lounge was so dark that it took her several seconds to adjust her eyes to it. At first she didn't spot him, and then she saw the smiling face and the nod of his head. She moved over to the small table in the corner and slid down opposite Frank. A sigh of total contentment rushed through her whole being as she looked into his eye.

Was it possible that she was in love with this man? Really in love with him?

Chapter Eight

The lodge had a large lobby with a massive stone fireplace at the far wall. Around the roaring fire were rustic wooden chairs, adding to the mood and atmosphere of the lodge's decorations. Gathered around the fire were a group of people, sitting, warming themselves by the hot flames, which crackled around the huge logs, and with the rich flavor and warmth of hot buttered rum, courtesy of the management.

The man sitting in the largest chair, nearest the fire, and surrounded by the others, was Karl Winter, his face a map of aged lines, humor and drama drawn on them from years of living and, one would guess, loving. He had the look of elder wisdom, a look that was added to by the large hand-carved pipe loosely clutched in his thin lips. The darkening eyes, so surrounded by the wrinkles of age as to give them an otherworldly look, twinkled brightly as they flashed from one person to another. This was his world, his creation and his little kingdom, into which he had put his life and his love for the last twelve years. It was a resting place for the young to experience something from a lost age, from a golden age of ease and hearty living. Karl Winter's was the local guru, the quite guardian of this immediate domain, his world, his place on the planet, his popular "classroom" where people came to listen. Here he was, in fact, simply a kindly old man sharing thoughts and ideas and, at times, even meaningful lessons learn during a long life well lived.

Jean MacManners watched him with intense interest. There was something about the man that caused her heart and mind to reach out with a tender loving embrace. He radiated a warmth and a restful feeling of contentedness, and she realized why she had been enjoying herself so much at the *Winter Lodge,* for he had created a glow the place, a feeling that couldn't be ignored, even though one hadn't met the man. Nobody could build something without having put their stamp of personality and philosophy of life on it. And, from what Jean had already seen, there was no doubt in her mind that this man believed in the relaxation of the soul and body, the releasing of love and kindly emotion. It was as if he had stamped it on every board and every nail and on every person that stepped into his *Winter* retreat. Everybody talked of the Old Man with a feeling of love and deep affection. There was a "private club" feeling about the people who stayed here, and she silently thanked Frank, with all her heart, for having brought her here to share the place with him. It was obviously special to all those present.

The conversation slowly dwindled down and somebody cried out, "Karl, how about a story?"

There were other requests and a hushed silence moved over the eager men and women.

Frank squeezed Jean's hand and smiled.

Karl Winter clasped his hands thoughtfully together and then, after a moment, reached for his pipe. He took out a tobacco pouch from his pocket and, emptying the pipe-bowl in the fireplace, refilled it, lighted it and puffed slowly. His lips smiled and all his face wrinkled brightly in response. A soft cough sounded from his throat and then he turned his aged eyes toward the audience, sweeping it completely.

"Well, now, what is it you want to hear!" His English *was* perfect, only slightly tainted with the mark of an accent.

There was silence, as if everybody knew that this was what he actually expected. They waited.

"You know sometimes an old man gets...well has the right to just sit and say...nothing."

There was a murmuring of disappointment

Karl Winter's eyes twinkled. Then his withered lips chuckled.

"Well, I guess that seeing all you young people so eager to hear an old man's ramblings...now, let me see."

He thought for a moment and then continued: "For some reason there comes to mind an event that happened so many years ago that...let's say it was before even the car existed. Before television and before planes and before radio, in that long gone world when all the pleasures came from what men could do by themselves, without outside, artificial help. Maybe seeing so many young couples here tonight reminds me."

A twinkle sparked in his eyes as he looked at the girls.

"This young lady—and lady she was, regardless of her rather sordid means of making a living—

came into my life when I was still in college—or rather, what you would now *call* college—at the *University of Heidelberg,* which is just off the Rhine.

"As you know in this time the idea of dueling was a mark of a man and you didn't get into the correct social circles unless you were in a dueling club. And this was the circle of friends with which I ran around. A duel would be started at the drop of a word, a drop of a mere thought or the drop of a slight insult—the insult didn't even have to apply to you, or even a friend of yours—the idea was to find some excuse to get into such an 'affair of honor.'

"Well, *it* so happened that one time we went out one evening for a little fun or, as we called it, *tolle Nacht,* which included the charms of a *leichte Mädchen.* We went to a place which was known to have such women for the price of a *Goldstucke* or less, depending on whom you would have. The young, dark-haired *Mädchen* who attracted my eye was plump and had a sensual beauty would attract many young men of my time. Her name was Megi Bottcher and we got along wonderfully. The prize for the evening was well worth the fare. She was a *Hure,* yet, I would rather have thought of her as a *Dirne,* and after that night I wished to think of her as something wonderfully special, since she was my first woman, and as is the folly of youth, my heart went out to her."

He paused and again his eyes moved to the women in the group. "I fear that I might have shocked you as to my ventures as a youth, if so please feel free to say so. But there is a point, which I shall make quite clear in a moment."

Nobody attempted to stop him.

He nodded, took a puff from his pipe and chuckled. "When I think about young men and the way young love can affect their minds and bodies and emotions...

"But Megi was more than just a *Hure*. She had an attractive charm that would appeal to any man or woman here. She wasn't cheap or vulgar—but rather had a classy behavior that lifted her far above her sisters in the profession.

"I returned many times to her and the fee dropped lower and lower until it consisted merely of a dinner and a bottle of wine in the privacy of her little room. We were in love. Fully and completely And for any man that falls in love for the first time—regardless with whom it might be—there is a special something about it.

"Megi was from a poor family, having lived in poverty all her life, her father dying when she was ten and her mother following a few years later. She was left with several younger sisters and brothers whom she helped support in the only way possible for a girl her age and with her lack of education. She disliked her profession—even more than most women who are forced into such a desperate activity for survival. She loved music, and we would go to the symphony any time it was possible. I had a minor income from my father, at the time, and we made the most of it. During that summer we enjoyed all the fruits of love and all the fruits of romance. It was perfection because first love is always a perfect thing, being round like a circle—it covers all and it encircles all, touching everything. The world becomes a glowing thing of rainbow colors, it bursts with life and birth—this was spring, and the beauty of my homeland was alive for the first time since I had been born. Of course, it wasn't any different, in reality, than any other year, but through the shine of love it had bloomed into a rosy paradise.

"I have gone into such detail merely to explain my feelings and to show how it was possible for the following events to come about. You must understand that, at this time, there was a deeply cut class line—and I was from a rich family. My friends, for the most part, looked upon the romance as that of a passing nature until one evening I returned to the university after a night with my Megi, to inform my friends that we were to be married. I was drunk with love and drunk from beer and wine. It had never occurred to me, up to this time, exactly what I'd gotten into. It was fully right to have such an affair, if one chose to, but it was socially impossible to let it evolve into something of a serious nature. You could be in 'love,' but not be serious about it. Such love, it is said, should be like the leaves of spring that bloom in gay colors and then slowly, as summer passes into autumn, they brown and then wither and fall to death. Nothing lasts; it merely momentarily springs to life, to fade at the proper season.

"Yet there was something within Megi which caused a man to desire to love and be loved for there was so much need in her for love and to love. She had never had real love until meeting me, and I'd never had love until meeting her—my *first* love. We were captured in our tide of emotions and found something which cried to be fulfilled, and I had asked her to marry me with all the honesty a young man can have at the time of his first affair—wanting to perfect it beyond reality.

"Well, as it was sure to happen, one of my friends made the honest mistake of trying to make me come down from the cloud of romantic ecstasy and see things as they actually were. He said in a fury of emotions: *'Sie ist eine dreckige Hure!'*— which is a crude way of calling her what she was—a cheap professional prostitute. But, he had chosen more vivid words to express his idea of what she was.

"As I pointed out at the beginning, a duel was something which could be started by a mere insult to somebody that didn't even mean anything to you—just an excuse to gain a few more scars of honor. I naturally challenged him right then, and there was no putting it off until the next day. I was wild with rage and hate, burning with insulted passion and *drunk!* A complete combination that leaves no room for subtitles. We went 'out back'—as you would call it nowadays.

"My friends tried to call it off—tried to talk sense to me—attempted to make me realize what a fool I was being for the *Dirne,* for I had yelled for blood, naked blades, stripped down to the waist— with no holds barred. I wanted blood and a lot of it to prove that no man could insult the woman of my love—regardless of what she was. I wanted the man's life. As it so happened, Weckesser was a very close friend and *didn't* want *my* life. Much to my luck, I might add. For in my state of physical confusion I could hardly handle a saber with any amount of skill—aside from the fact that my friend was a *very* skilled swordsman. I'd been pretty good myself, and never before had either of us fought together, so there was no way of knowing, for sure, who was the best—though it was fairly certain that I didn't have quite the ease and grace which my friend had with the weapon.

"There was small light from the moon and the stars and the darkness did little to help matters. We crossed swords, and in the next few moments my friend merely attempted to avoid my awkward attempts to cut off his head. It took little skill or effort on his part, but for myself I was exhausted before we'd been at it for more than a few moments. Those swords are hardly light, and in my condition I was lucky to even be able to last two minutes.

"But youth has muscles and I had anger to give me added strength. I kept swinging from left to right, aiming first at his head and then at his body!" His pipe was lightly swinging in the air to accent his story. "Then suddenly, by accident, I'm sure, for my friend had become quite careless by this time, my sword drew blood. Somebody shouted that honor had been satisfied and my friend dropped his sword point. I thrust home, cutting deep into his side. The wound *was* bloody and ugly, but not enough to stop his ability to use his own weapon. I guess he went momentarily mad with rage. That sword of his weaved such a pattern of thrusts and lunges and swings, nicking me, cutting me, and generally making things pretty bloody all around, that I sobered quite rapidly. The others surrounding us attempted to yell us apart, but it was much too late. The cuts had sharpened my mind and I began to become quite aware of the reality of what was happening.

"What fool are you? I asked myself. *Here you*

135

are, fighting for your life over a woman that has given her body to so many men that she has probably lost count—and she's still young at that!

"I quickly attempted to fend off my friend's sword, and at the same time tell him that it was over, that I was through, that I wished not to continue—that honor had been upheld on both sides. It was some time before he seemed to come out of his dazed anger and drop the point of his saber. After a moment, breathing heavily, staring at me, he smiled and then slowly fell forward onto the ground. It took him a week to get over the effects of the wound that I'd inflicted on him. It took me many months to get over the fact that I'd broken off relationships with Megi, and that she'd left for parts unknown. I still was in love with her."

He paused and thoughtfully puffed on his pipe, looking into the fire. Then he added: "I've often wondered what would have happened to me if I'd never entered into that duel. Would I have *really* married Megi? What changes would it have made in my life? Would the love have burned out in its own time—after autumn had dried up the leaves of my passion and let them fall to the ground of my past?" His eyes shifted to his silent audience.

"One never knows. But I did learn something as a result, which has stayed with me for the rest of my life: never let anything turn you away from going through with what you desire, for, in that turning away, you never know what would have happened and you never quite get over that *not* knowing. It is like being left up in the air, without a way of ever finding out where that path might have ended, if you had been allowed to follow it. In a blind alley—or would it have finally faded out? Or continued? I'll never know."

For a moment his eyes grew misty and then he smiled like old men many times smile, half amused and half sad, with the wisdom of age. "I've often wondered what happened to Megi."

For a long time nobody said anything, but stood there in a hypnotic daze.

Karl Winter broke the silence. "Well, that's my story, for this evening. You'll have to excuse me— an old man has to have his rest."

Jean had noticed a strange heaviness to the man's last words, and as he passed her, on his way through the crowd, she thought she saw moisture in his eyes, but she wasn't completely sure.

* * * * * * *

That evening, later, after several cocktails, Frank and Jean returned to their cabin. When the door had closed behind them, Jean turned to Frank.

"He's quite a man."

"Quite."

"I never knew that he would tell a story like *that!* He doesn't seem the kind that would."

"He's lived a long life, and he has a lot of stories like that."

"You think it's true?"

"I don't know. I imagine. Maybe colored by years but I've never seen him react like that before. I believe this one *was* true."

Jean was silent for a moment and then said: "It left me in a real mood."

"Most of his stories do leave the listener in a

mood. He never tells a story that doesn't have something of importance to reveal about human beings
and human nature."

"That part about never letting things hang—it
has a lot of implications," Jean remarked as they
moved into the bedroom and turned on the light.
"And I can't sort them all out! All I know is that he
was saying that you should grab hold of life and
hold on with all your strength, taking what it gives
and not turning away—letting it take you where it
will, without forcing or fighting." She hesitated,
added: "I wonder, too, what happened to Megi. I
feel sorry for her."

"*I* feel sorry for *myself*—you're not being very
attentive. Ever since Karl weaved his spell over you,
you haven't snapped out of it!" Frank laughed and
said, in a pleased voice: "But I'm glad you liked
him."

When Frank made love to her that evening, Jean
found a new meaning to his caress and her feelings
for him.

Was *this* merely a summer leaf that would
wither away when the autumn came, or was it something else, which would develop into a beautiful tree
of love? Or maybe a seed which was being planted
into the ground of her living experience, to sprout
into full bloom and finally into full life, to become
something of oneness and beauty! To make her
whole.

Jean didn't have much time to think about it,
because Frank's hands played over her body, developing a symphony of emotion and pleasure that rippled through every nerve.

It seemed that every erotic touch was a new kind

of pleasure out of which she experienced different, totally fresh thrilling response.

Every time his fingers played along he flesh she tensed all over. It all seemed new and wonderful, as if she were another woman who had never experienced sex with a man.

When his lips touched, kissed, then made love to her whole body, whole soul, the thrilling waves of joy that mounted her flesh were overwhelming. She felt weak all over and was only able to submissively respond, give herself totally to this wonderful man's lovemaking.

Jean clutched at the back of his neck, first in gentle passion, then caressing meaningfully. She gripped his thighs within the embrace of her legs, drawing him quickly to her again and again.

Then all at once they both strained together.

When this moment came, it was something more wonderful than it had ever been before. Something she couldn't even define, understand, because it was completely new in her life. The climax flooded over both of them and for a moment she felt as if attached mentally to this wonderful male. She was more a total part of him than she'd been of any other person.

Their very souls seem to blend in a mutual joy that made them one person.

For a long time they held one another, gasping, bathed in lover's sweat.

Her mind screamed: *Don't leave me, ever!*

It was madly insane passion, yet beautifully loving, because each of them had become totally responsive to the other's frantic need.

It was so different with Frank; and she felt the

difference in every way. And she felt a lovely contentment being with him.

"Oh, Frank, you're wonderful!" she murmured ever so softly.

"And you're fantastic! I've...never wanted a woman as much as I want to be a part of you."

She smiled up at him, said: "It is only sex, isn't it?"

But the look in his eyes suggested she was a foolish little girl if she believed that.

His body rolled away, lying next to Jean. She turned, curled up against him, his arm about her shoulders. She rested an exhausted hand against the flat expanse of his hard, muscular stomach, content in the male feel of this wonderful lover. That contact almost making them one.

It was a beautiful moment that flinted by, yet must have lasted for quite a while. She became aware of his even breathing and knew he'd fallen asleep.

Finally, she slipped away from his embrace, gently placing his arm at his side. Then lying back on the bed she bathed in the memory of their love-making, thrilled, yet slightly confused by her own thoughts.

It was some time before sleep finally started to soothe away thought. But when the blanket of sleep finally came it brought the nightmares again to pervert her rest, distort the loving beauty she'd experienced in Frank's arms.

She was standing on a cliff, overlooking a shore of white sand, the ocean roaring below, slashing up on to the beach and around the leaping feet of the two swordsmen below.

Each was naked from the waist up, one female and the other male. The woman's breasts move rhythmically with every thrust and swing of her sword. The man's muscles rippled as he fended off the flashing blade with his own weapon.

"Stop! Stop!" Jean screamed, leaping over the edge of the cliff, floating gracefully downward toward the fighting couple. "Frank—Debbie! Stop. Don't!"

Neither of them paid any attention to Jean. They continued to slash out at each other, hatred distorting their faces.

To Jean's horror she saw Frank's blade dip deep into Debra's chest as he, at the same time, doubled over in agony with the woman's sword cutting through his groin.

But they didn't stop. Frantically they swung their weapons at each other, and Jean, in desperation, leaped between them. The two weapons began slicing into her, bringing deep terrible wounds to her flesh, covering it with the crimson of her own blood.

Jean jerked up in bed, screaming, "Stop! Stop! You're killing me! You're killing me—you're killing me..." The words choked in her throat, sweat broke out over her body.

"What's wrong?" Frank cried, alarmed, sitting up in bed and hurriedly placing an arm tenderly around her shoulder. "It's all right. What's wrong? You must have been dreaming. Jean—take it easy."

Slowly, she quieted, leaning against Frank. A shudder rushed through her and she felt a terrible panic. Sleep wasn't giving her rest—it was only giving horror and exhaustion. It was a long time before she could relax her breathing and calm the pounding rhythm of her heart.

"Want to talk about it?" Frank asked, gently.

"No. Not now." *Not ever,* she added to herself. *She could never tell anybody about the horror of her nightmares. Never!*

After a long time they moved apart and she lay quietly, aware of the man going to sleep next to her, but not finding sleep for herself. Jean was afraid of what dreams might come, and for the rest of the night she lay there in a tight convulsion of thoughts and terrors and guilt, until dawn came and with it the light of the new fresh day.

She got up from bed and moved into the bathroom and showered. Afterwards, she went into the living a room and waited for Frank to awake.

* * * * * * *

The long drive back to Los Angeles was heavy with silence. Frank seemed to sense that Jean's mood wasn't merely depression.

Her thoughts raged, savagely, confused, agonized.

How did she really feel about Frank? How could she really feel anything for him, so soon? Should she run from him before the mounting conflict had come to the point where the need for both Frank and Debra had destroyed her?

What about Debra? Was she the "Megi" in her life? The one who would always be that element of the unknown to plague her for the rest of her life?

Or was it Frank a new love to surrender to?

She didn't know Frank long enough to be cer-

142

tain about his importance in her life, his role as a "Megi"—but Debra certainly could be considered such an issue to be resolved one way or the other before going on to a next serious emotional commitment.

And she had thought leaving New York had done just that. But, apparently, Debra hung there in the back of her mind like an obsessive demon, a continual nightmare.

She had run from Debra in terrible confusion, determined to wash the woman out of her mind. Yet she remained a frightening factor that simply wouldn't go away.

It was a couple of hours before she actually got around to any form of conversation with Frank. No answer had come to her, but one thought had burst into being: she should get a job and an apartment, immediately.

"Frank, you offered me a job and I said I'd consider you first. Well—"

"You'll take it?" Frank's voice was alive with eagerness.

"No! Not that one. Joe offered me one the other evening, too. But I won't take it, either. I want something away from friends and relatives." She hesitated. "I thought maybe you might know something."

"I'll think about it."

He was silently thoughtful for a long time and then made a suggestion. "There's a man—Ben Temple—who might be able to get you something with *Life Insurance*. How soon do you want to know?"

"Soon as possible. The sooner I get away from

staying with Mary and Joe, the better."

Several hours later they arrived at the Hanson home. Frank just dropped her off and when she went in she found that Mary was still silently depressed, still distant. She decided to ignore it.

"There's a letter for you from New York," Mary told her in a tight, dead voice, her eyes blank of emotion. "On your bed."

Jean felt a hardness inside her, a tight fear. Quickly she went into the bedroom, closed the door, dropped her luggage on the floor and picked up the envelope.

For a long time she just stared at it. The handwriting was Debra's. The only thing that caused her to finally open it was the realization that the longer she waited the worse it would get.

In Debra's flowing, beautiful handwriting, the letter read:

"Dear Jean.

"How are you? I've missed you so very much. You don't know. It seems that I can't get you out of my mind. Why did you have to leave me like you did? There seems nothing in the world of importance for me, now. I think of the way we—but I don't want to think about that right now.

"Is there any *hope that you might return?*

"What have you been doing there? Found any social activity? I hope that you have been thinking about me, I

144

miss you so much!

"I thought it would be possible to say so many things to you, yet I find that the words are difficult. Just sitting here and writing...

"Don't forget what I've told you about us.

"There is nothing wrong in being the way we are.

"Only society says so—but who is society? Men!

"A man's world, and men don't like the idea of women loving women! Unless it is for some perverted stag-film! Such disgusting creatures they are!

"But there's nothing wrong with our kind of love. It is pure and directly honest. Why shouldn't we have the right to be ourselves? Why shouldn't we have the right to enjoy the way we are? Why should we be forced to hide our true nature, true feelings, and needs, from society?

"So we're different, but isn't everybody in the world different in one way or another? Doesn't everybody have some stamp of personality that is different from others? From the cruel, judgmental world. Bigots and mindless, cruel bastards that somehow have convinced themselves they had the right to dictate their moral concepts on everybody else, no matter how wrong they

are in reality.

"If I only had been a different kind of woman then maybe I could have held you longer—proven to you what it could be like. How wonderful it can be when two women love each other the way we did. No man can really know how a woman feels; no man can ever really understand a woman's needs the way a woman can. No man knows how to love like a woman. With gentle tenderness and full understanding. With a oneness that is as complete as we had together. We understood each other and we were eager to please and give. A man only wants a woman's body, and a woman to clean his home and take care of him and say 'yes, sir, anything you want, sir!' because he wants to feel he's superior and better than a woman; and he tries to prove it all the time—because he's nothing, and knows it—he's just an animal with base animal desires. He can think of nothing but how many women he has had—how many more he can have!

"He doesn't know the bare meaning of loyalty and love—love to him is merely taking a woman's body and then another woman's body, just to prove that he's a man! Is that the kind of life you want? To be nothing more than a hole to satisfy a man's need for orgasm?

146

"A life where you never know if the man will come home and be with you— or be out with some other woman? They never can be trusted!

"The kind of life that never is sure of itself

"The kind of life which keeps you in an inferior position—never quite accepted as a mental equal—something which he will call 'sweet little one' or 'you little darling.' which really means that he is only thinking that you are something to take care of and play with. A toy. A mere plaything—which he buys, because he pays for your food and home!

"Isn't that just like prostitution? That's what it is! You sell your body— being owned—but not loved! There is no love in a man—not the kind of wonderful and understanding and giving perfection there is between two women who know and understand and share with each other!

"With us it was so wonderfully perfect! We shared! We helped each other, and gave to each other. We weren't 'kept!' women. We were equal in all things! We were thoughtful! We were— oh, it's terrible to just think about it! It hurts so very much to think about it!

"My whole soul burns for you—my body desires only your nearness. Everything, every thought within me, is

centered on you.

"It's so hard to be here, with you there—so far away. If only you were near, so that I could tell my side of the story and keep you on the right level, so that the men won't talk you into something bad and wrong! It is so difficult for me!!!!

"Men are evil—never forget that! They only want things for themselves! They don't love and couldn't love anybody but themselves.

"Oh, Jean—just remember that I'm waiting. Remember that, and maybe you'll come back to me. When that time comes, and I'm sure that it must, I'll send you the money to return. What man would do the same? After what has happened between us? What man's ego would allow him to do it?

"I love you desperately! Never forget that. And I'll be waiting for you, with all my heart.

"Love, oh, so much love and love and love,

> *"Forever yours,*
> *"Debbie."*

Jean folded up the letter very neatly and then collapsed on the bed. For a long time she lay there trying hard not to think about Debra's words; trying not to let them affect her emotionally or mentally. They were confusing thoughts, ideas, pleas.

It wasn't right to listen to such words, she told herself. Yet, as the moments passed, they kept burning into her mind like hot pincers, making their branding mark.

"Oh, Debbie, I do need you. You're the only person that I could ever talk to!" her mind cried out in desperation, the words softly forming on her lips.

The need to be able to talk to somebody who would truly understand her frustrations and pains and sorrows was so strong within Jean that she found it hard to control the impulse to pack all her belongings and hurriedly return to New York on the next flight out.

It would be an easy matter to pick up a phone and call Debra, to hear the woman's voice.

No. Never! Her mind rebelled at the very thought. *That's the last thing in the world I need!*

Jean suddenly found herself walking out of the room. This time she didn't forget to take her purse. She walked down the street toward Pico. It would be a long walk to the first bar, but the need to find escape, to find some means of running from her thoughts, was now overpowering.

Finally she came to Pico and turned west. There was a bar down the street. She walked in to find mental oblivion.

* * * * * * *

Mary Hanson watched Jean leave the house with an inner relief. Ever since that night Joe had forcefully seduced her, and caused such wild feelings to overwhelm every nerve and muscle in her body, Mary had felt a deep inner guilt and—concern and

fear about herself, fear that maybe there was something wrong. And her hate for Jean had grown—
because there *was* something wrong with *her!*

For several hours she didn't give in to the impulse to enter Jean's room and search it. But there
was a need to understand what had happened; what
had caused her sister to leave the house without
even a good-bye. She knew that it must involve the
letter which Mary was sure had come from Jean's
New York Lesbian lover. It had been difficult to
even touch the letter. Finally, it was impossible to
restrain the urge to know something more about her
sister, even while feeling guilty about it. She
stepped into Jean's room, saw the folded letter on
the bed where Jean had left it. For only a moment
Mary hesitated, then reached out and picked it up,
carefully opening and reading it.

When she was finished she found herself wanting to throw up. That any woman could say things
like that, could be like that, made her violently sick.
That her own sister could be like "that" was even
worse. Mary decided to let Joe read the letter. That
would be best; let him know the truth.

What Mary didn't know was that her own fears
about herself were moving her to destroy somebody
else, close to her—and Jean MacManners was the
number one choice.

When Joe came home from golf Mary told him
about Jean and how she had rushed off without any
explanation.

"I found this on her bed. I know—it wasn't right
for me to read it—but, well, I was concerned about
her! Now—now, I think you should read it."

The bitterness in his wife's voice caused him to

150

take the letter.

Disgust exploded through Joe when he had finished reading.

He turned to Mary and said, "I think you were right, reading it. When she returns, tell her she has to leave. I don't want any woman like *that* in my house! *And that's final!*"

Mary felt an inner glow, something she didn't quite understand, but something that made her feel good inside.

Later, when Frank Martin called, asking to speak to Jean, Joe managed to mention the letter. There was a long silence after Frank had heard that it was from Jean's Lesbian lover, and then his voice sighed through the receiver, and the line went dead.

Chapter Nine

Frank stood by the phone for a long time thinking about what Joe Hanson had told him. It didn't seem possible that a woman like Jean could be a Lesbian. She had responded like a normally developed woman with very female desires; yet he realized that it was fully possible that she was putting on an act. Some women could fake it so skillfully that nobody would guess the truth. After a long time he refused to think anything more about it. This wasn't his problem, and he had at least enjoyed himself as a result of having known Jean MacManners.

While he was fixing a steak for dinner he heard the front doorbell ringing.

"Be there in a moment!" he called, turning off the fire under the skillet. Stepping to the door he opened it and then jerked back in surprise.

Jean was standing there, her eyes bright and her hair slightly messed. For a moment she weaved drunkenly, and then started to stagger forward.

Frank hurriedly caught her. The softness of her body caused an electric desire to race through him. He tried to ignore it.

"What's wrong?" he asked, startled at her being there. Plus feeling mixed emotions ravage through

152

his whole mind and body.

"Shothing!" she slurred.

Closing the door, he helped Jean onto the living room couch. "You need some coffee."

Jean merely grinned, then after a moment of looking up into his eyes, she announced, "I want you!"

The words had come out very slowly and carefully, as if she were struggling to control them.

Physical impulse almost caused Frank to reach for Jean and take that lovely body to his. Then he remembered Joe's words: *Jean's a Lesbian. She has a female lover in New York!*

Frank stepped back in horror, trying to fight off the inner disgust, but finding it impossible. He stared down at Jean as if she were some ugly animal with a deadly disease.

"What're you doing here?"

"Swat shu mean?" she demanded, her face struggling, her eyes seeming to have difficulty focusing on him.

"You here for kicks? Is that it?" The words burst out of Frank's mouth with contempt and anger. "What'd you go out with me for? Kicks? To find out if it was any different from woman? Is that what you wanted to know? You get your kicks out of seeing a man go crazy with physical desire for you?"

"What?" Suddenly her face seemed more sober. She shook her head and stared savagely at him. "What you talking 'bout?"

"I found out about you. You and your girl friend in New York. What was I for…just a lark? Well, I'll have you know you were just for kicks, too. Just a cute little lay!"

Jean stared at him for a long time and then her lips slowly clamped tight; her eyes went stony, cold.

"How?" she asked in a dead voice.

"Joe saw the letter you got from your…lover." Frank turned away, disgusted, stepping across the room, picked up a pack of cigarettes. He felt sick. His hands shook as he lighted a cigarette.

There was a long silence and then he heard Jean standing and moving across the room toward the front door.

"It wasn't for kicks. Frank. But thanks—for *nothing!*" The door opened and then slammed shut.

Frank raised his cigarette and took a deep drag. A mixture of relief and depression fluttered through him.

Why should he care?

But he knew the answer to that one: *He'd been getting really serious about Jean MacManners.*

That's a laugh on you, buster! Fell for a Lesbian!

Shrugging angrily, he went to the phone and called Kay Clifford.

"Hello?" her voice sounded over the receiver.

"Frank here. Are you free tonight?" was his direct, simple question.

"Gee, Frankie, I don't know about that!" Her voice was light, throaty. "Such short notice. I have such a busy schedule. And normally I've very expensive, you know. Seldom free!"

"Well? Are you or aren't you?" he almost snarled.

"Well, don't bite my head off, honey. I'm always free for you!"

"Then I'll be there soon."

154

"How soon?"

"Within the hour too soon?"

"Well, I don't know if I have anything decent to wear."

"Why be decent?" he countered, almost cheerfully.

"Oh, so you're in one of your moods?"

"My moods?"

"Well, I bet you'd be simply delighted to find me with nothing on at all!"

"How'd you guess?"

"Oh, you men. All the same. Want a woman hot and bothered and stripped, ready to charge wildly into your arms. Is that about it?"

"Well, to be truthful, that would certainly be a delightful surprise. Even if I hadn't thought about that."

"Oh, sure. It never crossed your mind! I'll be waitin' for you, all a-pantin' and eager to envelope my lovely man within my evil, wanton embrace. And right down and dirty where it does us the most good! I can promise you that…surprise!" She paused long enough to simply let that sink in, then added: "Is that good enough for you?"

He simply said: "Perfect!"

"I'll be here, all hot and bothered!" she promised, and then the line went dead.

A surge of real raw animal desire rushed through him.

It'll be good having a real woman, he thought, returning to the kitchen and his steak. *A real hot, delicious, overwhelmingly charged woman who couldn't get enough of a real man.* No holds barred, no restrictions; and most of all, no perverse past

155

other than a string of male lovers to satisfy her endless sexual needs.

Yes, Kay was perfect! Just the kind of wild evening he needed

* * * * * * *

Jean walked for a long time, bitterness tight in her mind. But no collective thoughts were centering themselves into any logical pattern. Only the awareness that everything was finished and that she would have to leave the Hansons right away, regardless. Then she realized it would be impossible to face them, even to pack her things together. The only thing left was to find some place to stay the night, and then call Mary to have her personal belongings delivered to wherever she was.

After about half an hour of walking aimlessly, Jean spotted a phone booth, mentally noted what cross streets she was at, and then phoned for a taxi. When it came she told the driver to take her to a hotel. "An inexpensive one."

An hour later, Jean was in a small, dingy room, a bottle on the stand next to her. The bed was lumpy, but she didn't care.

Her mind was functioning a little more clearly and it was heavily bathed in self-pity.

You feel damned sorry for yourself, Jean, she thought. *But you have good reasons! Don't you?*

What a fool you were, you almost fell in love with that dirty, no-good male slob. The bastard! What right did he have to talk that way to you?

Then her mind turned to her sister and brother-in-law and she saw where the real blame was. They hadn't had a right to look at her mail. Yet, she admitted, the mistake was her own! She shouldn't have left an open letter where anybody could pick it up to read.

Where now, little girl? she asked herself bitterly. *Where now?*

A job. Work, and find some kind of existence for yourself! That's the best thing you can do. Find some kind of normal life—with or without a man or woman.

Sleep finally came to her drunken mind and body, but not without her having come to one conclusion: she had already fallen in love with Frank Martin regardless of everything else. She had fallen in love and he had become her "Megi."

Strangely, she didn't find it odd that her thoughts hadn't centered around Debra. Only one thought came to her mind about Debra Channings. *She would think about that the next day; think and try to understand why it was that suddenly she didn't I have any emotional feelings for the woman; no feelings at all!*

Chapter Ten

Frank buried his face into the softness of Kay's breasts, feeling a dizzy, wild excitement and pleasure in the act. It was the first time in weeks that he had actually found such a deep physical pleasure with Kay. Her wild passion, hunger for him had washed away the bitterness and hurt hammered home upon finding out about Jean MacManners.

"You're lovely, Kay," he whispered, throatily.

She trembled under him and a deep sigh came from her parted lips. "I love you, Frankie."

He ignored the remark, knowing that Kay wasn't the kind that loved a man for very long. He caressed her breasts with his lips and tongue and explored her silken flesh with his hands, covering her body with touches, which caused it to squirm in eager response.

"Don't wait, honey," she whispered, clawing at him, drawing him down to her. "Don't wait."

He didn't wait. Didn't care about anything but being consumed totally by this wonderfully passionate, wild woman.

Forcefully, he thrust her thighs apart and she sobbed, writhing at their very first contact.

He continued until the flood of sexual release exploded deep within her. As he withdrew, she

158

leaped up, taking him in her hands, squeezing and fondling.

"God, its good to me. I just love it violent like that!"

He chuckled slightly, but didn't really feel any great sense of pleasure at her words. Just a sense of momentary release. Emotionally it was all meaningless.

"You're a good woman, Kay!"

Her hands were idly stroking him and it felt pleasant, though he wasn't ready to fully respond.

"Get that thing hard, Frank!" she pleaded. "I'm still hot for it! Makes me feel so hot!"

"Help yourself!" Frank offered.

"I'll make you real hard!" she promised, slipping down full length on top of him. Slowly, she lifted and lowered her hips, up and down, sensually caressing him.

"Does that feel good?" Kay asked.

"What do you think?"

"Tell me how good it feels!"

"Shut up and just do your stuff!" he demanded, nastily.

"You're in a strange mood, lover!" Kay observed, wiggling her hips lightly back and forth.

"I'm in a mood, all right!" Frank assured her, reaching down and gripping her fanny with both hands. He absently squeezed the molded flesh, only vaguely aware of any real pleasure. It was all automatic, driven by a very real need to stop thinking about anything else.

She moaned in pleasure. "That feels good! I'm very sensitive in my fanny."

"You're sensitive all over!"

"No, I mean it. I just *love* being spanked." The tone of her voice was open invitation.

He lightly slapped her.

"Oh, do that again, but much harder!" she pleaded.

Raising his hand, he slapped it down on her fanny and she moaned in pleasure.

"Much harder, Frank!"

Automatically, without thinking, he hit her again, this time almost as hard as he could, feeling a sense of pleasure at doing so, though not considering the reason for this reaction.

She gasped, her hips surged wildly against him in such an erotic way that he felt himself go rigid all over.

"You're getting hard," she observed a moment later. "I just love being spanked like that. Do it some more, love."

Impulsively, Frank sat up, pulling her across his thighs. Then he struck her fanny. The sound of impact was loud; like the sharp crack of a log being broken in two.

"Oh Frank, that hurts so beautifully!"

And with each blow, Kay writhed voluptuously.

Something inside him both rebelled and thrilled to what was happening. It gave him some kind of perverted release, hitting Kay—though he had the vague idea she represented a kind of universal female—without real identity of her own.

He thought about Jean and his hand struck down harder against Kay's fanny.

She almost screamed in pain.

"Enough, enough. I want you in me!" She attempted to get away from him, but Frank was hitting her fanny again and again, harder and harder; almost insanely.

Finally she was crying, sobbing, but her body continued to writhe, convulsively responding.

All at once Frank came out of his sudden rage and daze enough to release her.

Kay clawed all over him, throwing his body down on the bed. She straddled his hips and he was aware of the most fantastically orgiastic look of lust in her eyes.

Then her hips started grinding away like some insane machine.

It wasn't gentle and it wasn't even nice, but the wildness of her sexual attack was overwhelmingly exciting for its raw, wild abandon. She screeched in open joy, utterly insanely out of her mind in the pleasure of it all. There was no doubt that Kay being all female, wanting a man totally captured inside her, wanting to know the thrilling sensation of normal, unrestraint union.

When he'd reached the end of his rope, his voice cried out. His lips uttered the one word they shouldn't have, which caused the woman to stiffen like a rigid log.

"Jean!"

They both froze for an instant—then Kay assaulted him more wildly with her hips, bringing on a quick, orgiastic climax. When she lifted away, Frank was floating in a mental daze, confused, painfully aware that his climax had been for Jean—not Kay.

He had desperately wanted it to be Jean who had so totally spent his passions inside her, not Kay.

The woman laid there beside him, silent, unmoving; still and thoughtful, her eyes tightly closed.

There had been a lot of pleasure given by Kay's body—but his mental image of Jean convulsing beneath his had been overwhelming.

Thoughtfully, Frank reached for a cigarette on the nightstand next to the bed. He lighted it and took a deep drag.

The woman lying next to him didn't stir, but there were tears glistening in her eyes, which had opened as he moved. But he wasn't even aware of Kay being there any more.

How could a woman like Jean have found pleasure in another woman's caresses? What illicit desire was plaguing her that caused her to seek out such degenerate pleasure?

He lay there and continued to wonder and the memory of Karl Winter's story suddenly burst into full meaning to his mind. That old man who had seemed untouched by anything, any more, had felt an emotional reaction in remembering his "Megi," and had left to be alone, to think about that woman who was no doubt now already long in her grave. Had that been the man's only *true* love?

Frank wondered how he felt about Jean? Did he love her, regardless of everything?

That thought had a double impact. The mere fact that he so easily accepted the idea that he was in love with a woman whom he hardly knew, and that he was even in love with *anybody,* except himself, jarred Frank.

All his life, Frank had merely taken what was offered, never thinking about where he was going or where it would end. Just that he did no real harm to anybody. Now he began to wonder. About everything.

You own a part interest in a business—you work your ass off and lay anything with a skirt that'll take it off for you!

But was he finding any meaning or reward out of life? All his thoughts had centered on how many "chicks" he could get. How long would that last? And when would it turn to mere loneliness? Would he end up with an inner pain about not having fought for what he really wanted?

Jean had run from New York.

Why?

And had gone out with him.

Why?

Frank knew that it was possible for a woman to fall into a relationship with a Lesbian and still desire men.

He suddenly realized what it was that had bothered him. It had been Kay's reactions to his touches and lovemaking that had caused him to think about Jean.

Jean had reacted much the same way.

Abruptly, Frank knew what he had to do. Find Jean, and try to make her understand that it didn't make any difference to him what she had done in the past, that the only thing that mattered was what she did in the present and the future. Frank didn't know what would happen if he continued to go out with Jean, and he didn't care, right then. But he knew it would be necessary to find out what Jean could possibly mean to him. To let things work out. Let events take him where they would.

He turned to Kay, letting his eyes rove over her still uncovered body. She was a wonderfully built woman; and knew how to use her body. He knew that he could now make love to her again, but in a much different way; not the way which was mere escape from himself and his inner feelings.

He reached for her and covered her lips with light, tender kisses. She responded, reluctantly at first, and then with a wild, heated passion.

* * * * * * *

It was around eleven o'clock that the luggage came to the *Fairmont Hotel,* where Jean had spent the night. She signed for it and then checked out of the hotel. What little money she had would last a couple of weeks.

The rest of the day she spent getting a small apartment, and after that, going to an employment agency. There were several job offerings for a girl who had experience as a secretary. She got the addresses of those places and went to one of them. The price offered for her services wasn't enough for the job being offered. Sixty-five dollars a week for a woman who had made five hundred dollars a month was too much of a drop. Jean returned home and fixed herself a drink.

That evening she went to bed early, unaware of the fact that Frank Martin had spent an hour trying to locate her, first by calling Mary Hanson, who had given the address of the hotel where Jean's luggage had been sent, and then by rushing to the hotel, only to discover that she had already checked out.

Jean thought about Frank, and thought about the mess she had made of her life. She thought about herself and she thought shortly about Debra. Memory of that letter had caused her to realize the terrible, distorted lies Debra had written. Men weren't the way Debra painted them to be. She had merely stated the typical attitude some Lesbians often expressed. Jean knew that men could be tender and wonderful.

She dropped the thought of Debra and took another drink.

* * * * * * *

The next morning she found a job that paid $115 a week. The position was that of private secretary to an older man who was happily married and had several grown children. As much as employers had been interviewing her, Jean had been returning the favor. She had felt it important to find somebody who wouldn't be making passes. She wanted to stay away from any entanglements. She needed a lot of time to think, without any friends or family interfering.

Several weeks later she had a phone put in her apartment. She had gotten almost to where she didn't think too much about Frank. But when thoughts of him did return to plague her mind, a depression settled there and she would get roaring drunk, alone in the apartment where nobody could see her agony.

Then one evening, when she was starting dinner, the phone rang.

She automatically assumed it was her boss. But as she picked up the receiver another man's voice said, "Hello, Jean?"

For a moment she didn't even think of Frank

Martin; he was the last person in the world from whom she would have expected to receive a call.

"This is Frank," the voice continued, before she could answer. "Have you forgotten, already?"

Her first impulse was to slam the receiver down, and then something made her pause.

"What do you want?" she demanded icily.

"Thank goodness. I've been trying to get you for weeks. I'd given up, until I thought about looking for a phone number, just on the chance you'd gotten one."

"What is it you want, Frank?" she asked coldly. But her heart was suddenly pounding inside her chest and her breath was tightly caught in a hard ball deep in her throat.

"Wanted to see you."

"For what? For 'kicks'?"

There was a moment's silence and then he said, "I guess I have that coming."

"Don't you know when it's finished?" she demanded.

"I don't!" Frank shouted, emotionally. "I haven't been able to get you off my mind."

"Because I'm such a good lay?"

"Cut it out, Jean. Give me a chance!" he pleaded. "So I said a few things I shouldn't have—it was quite a shot in the head...it was a little bit of a surprise, what Joe told me, and I'd not adjusted to it, or given it much thought. I've thought it over and I don't think it makes any difference."

"I think it does," Jean said. "I don't think you would ever forget."

She paused and then slowly hung up the phone without another word. Standing there for a long time

166

she thought about what Frank was offering. Maybe he realized that women could get caught in a trap and not be able to find an easy way out. Maybe he had realized she wasn't really any different from other women. Or, on the other hand—she didn't want to think about that. The idea that he might be merely interested in playing her along for fun, for kicks, was too cruel to think about.

Slowly going into the kitchenette, Jean turned the little hot plate off and reached for the bottle in the cupboard. She wanted to get roaring drunk and not think about what had just happened.

The first drink merely soothed her emotions.

The second began to work on them.

The third began to work on her body.

Suddenly, she realized that drinking by herself wouldn't help. Also, drinking was only the beginning. There had to be something else, something more fulfilling. With a defeated sigh she realized what was necessary.

Go out and find a man to be with. She didn't have to go anyplace with him; she didn't have to submit to some sordid sexual interplay in a cheap, crummy hotel room. All she needed to do was find something that would give her some release from the tormented thoughts shoving through her mind and emotions. Maybe just some companionship; company.

She half convinced herself that there wasn't a chance in hell she'd pick up some guy and go off with him for a sexual interlude.

There was a place where she had spent a couple of evenings and had been approached by men. In a little less than half an hour she had settled herself onto a barstool in the dimly lighted *Rocking Horse Bar & Grill*. The place was mostly "bar" with little "grill." By nine there would be a small combo to play Western rock and roll and go-go country music. It was one of those typical social-club pickup joints where young girls came to look down their noses at the men trying to pick them up. But there were a few, like herself, who simply didn't want to be alone; who wanted a man; and those women always managed to get what they were after: conversation, a drink, dancing and some party in private, elsewhere.

Jean sipped the martini and thought about her future. There wasn't really much to look forward to, except to continue the life she had now started. Work and maybe find a man—one like Frank. Maybe get married. Have children.

She took another sip of the martini and then, after looking into the glass, downed it, ordered another and waited.

It was nine-thirty by the time the musicians had started playing their noisy music. She was now already on her fourth cocktail, feeling lightly drunk. She had been looking around at the other customers who had come into the place, and one man had attracted her attention. He looked several times in her direction and smiled. After the second number from the bandstand, he stood and moved over to her.

"Want to dance?" he inquired in a pleasant voice.

Jean smiled. "Why not?"

As they walked to the dance floor, a rhythm number broke the silence and the man started the contortions that made his body seem obscene, his lips grinning, his eyes locked heatedly to hers.

Jean didn't really feel anything for the man, but she had already made up her mind that if he wanted to go some quiet place, she would take up his offer. After the music stopped they stood there for a moment and then Jean said, "Why don't we sit down?"

The man stared at her and shrugged. "Anything you like."

They moved back to the bar and he took the stool next to hers. "Can I buy you a drink?"

"Why not?" Jean nodded. "I could use one." She quickly finished what was left of her martini. There was a moment of silence until the bartender could get to them. After drinks were ordered the man turned and introduced himself. "Sam—that's my name. How 'bout yours?"

"Jean."

"Okay, now we're friends." He hesitated and then continued, "I haven't seen you around here before."

"Just a couple of times."

"Thought so. Would have noticed. I usually hang around here on the weekends, and sometimes during weeknights, like now."

The drinks arrived and Jean was thankful to start working on hers. The mixture of excitement and inner guilt about what she was doing needed a little more alcoholic buzz.

"You live around here?" Sam asked.

"Not too far away," she managed to say, feeling a nervous tightness dig at her stomach.

It's coming, she thought, *it's coming pretty soon now.*

"I live a couple of miles away. Nice place."

169

There was an awkward silence.

Jean sipped her cocktail, trying to find something to do or say.

"I never stay here long—can't take the music. Don't get me wrong—"

"I don't," she put in.

"I like it. But take it in small doses. But there's not many places a man and woman can get to know each other."

For a moment Jean had a feeling she wanted to run. Then she said, "1 know what you mean."

"You feel the same way about it?"

"Doesn't everybody?" she inquired, avoiding his question.

There was a short silence after that.

"You planning on staying long?" Sam asked.

"Where?" The question had startled Jean, and she jerked her head in his direction.

"Here."

"Oh, I don't know. Came in for a drink." She quickly added, "And to see what there was to see."

The implication of her statement wasn't missed. They sat quietly for a long time. She finished her drink. Boldness finally replaced nervousness. The liquor had worked its effect over her.

She turned, faced him, said: "Why don't we go someplace else?"

Sam seemed startled by her offer. But she didn't care a damn about Sam—or anyone else, or what they might think.

"Sure, sure, lady!" Sam exclaimed. "Let's get out of this dump!"

Sam paid for the drinks and they quietly moved through the thickening crowd on the dance floor and finally out of the building. They stood on the street for a moment and then Sam took hold of her arm, leading her toward a car parked a few yards down the street. Once inside, he slipped close to Jean and pulled her into his arms. His lips were open and moist and she returned the kiss with a wildness and hunger that startled her. It excited Jean much more than she would have thought possible; in a moment she knew why: it had been such a long time. And she needed to rediscover herself as a woman with a man. She needed to find out the truth. She felt breathless as they parted.

"You want to go someplace private?" Sam offered.

"What do you think?"

Jean was trying hard to make herself light-hearted about what was happening; yet a nervousness and guilt kept plaguing her. It wasn't that she hadn't let herself be picked up before; but for some reason it all seemed so shallow, so empty, without any emotional content.

Stop thinking, she told herself. *Stop thinking and just live for the moment. Experience. Live, girl! Live!*

Sam started the car and directed it down the street, cruising, his eyes keeping alert for a motel. At the first one he pulled the car to the side of the road. "This okay?"

Jean nodded, holding down her anxiety. She kept telling herself that she had to be with a man, repeating it over and over in her mind, until she was slowly driving her guilt away. But not quite. It was her new mantra. Everything seemed to remind her of other times she had been in a motel or "private place" with a "lover." First with her married "lover," then with her Lesbian "lover," and then with Frank Martin.

Sam went to the office and then returned and helped her out of the car. The drinks were dizzy in her brain, playing there like happy little fingers.

Finally, they stepped into the small, cheap motel room and the door closed behind them.

"Well, not much of a place," Sam admitted, "but it'll serve its purpose."

The statement chilled Jean, but already the mood had begun to overcome her reluctance. What she was doing might be wrong from a socially acceptable point of view, but she'd done many things in the past of which she wasn't proud. A person had to live from day to day and find what happiness there was to find. Life wasn't the storybook adventure and romance most people would like to believe. It was cold reality, with loneliness and physical and emotional needs which an adult body and mind couldn't ignore.

What happened next was a mixture of acts that horrified and at the same time thrilled her. A part of her mind was totally fascinated by what was happening, and another part was disgusted. He was an animal; a pig; yet so powerfully demanding that it was overwhelming a basic element inside her that was unable to resist.

Sam reached for Jean. His touch, and the way he roughly yanked her to him, had a forcefulness that left no room for hesitation. His lips found hers and they were moist and parted. The kiss was lingering and his hand started roving over her breasts, sinking deep. She felt his lungs heaving and the stale taste

172

of his mouth created a repellent reaction through her—but the physical need and the desperation which had brought her here had pushed her passions far beyond the point of allowing anything to stand in her way. She didn't care any more; no thoughts or restraint plagued her; no guilt tormented her mind. She had suddenly become the base animal the man wanted her to be.

Sam pulled up Jean's dress, then lowered her panties. His hand cupped her crotch.

He chuckled in delight, saying, "You have a cute little kitty-cat down there, baby!"

She moved her hips, invitingly, feeling wicked and sense of unrestraint animal joy. This was raw, basic sex, without any sense of caring. All that counted was allowing physical pleasure to dance into reality, into being, and then simply riding with the momentary thrills. There was nothing pretty about what was taking place. It was raw, dirty, cheap; voluptuous in its intense vulgar actions.

One hand pawed her breast, almost hurting.

"I have it ready for you, baby!" he told her.

Her hands reached between his legs, opened his zipper. He was almost frighteningly huge.

"Come on, baby, don't jack it off!" Sam gasped in pleasure.

"What do you want?" she inquired, suddenly without much excitement. A part of her was hot for him, but the rest was icy cold, almost terrified at what was happening. It was like dreaming, like a nightmare and a part of her just watched, detached, not really believing what was happening. It felt like a scene from some movie. These were other people acting out some strange scene. Yet she felt the sensations.

He urged her to the bed, and then roughly tossed her backwards, lifting her skirt, then yanking off her panties. A moment later he forcefully shoved himself down in one brutalizing stroke.

She almost screamed in pain, but in moments her body to begin responding. It was overwhelming, and with every rapid rabbit-like stroke she felt a kind of wildly perverted thrill at being taken so crudely—being almost raped by a savage beast.

And after that, everything seemed to blend into a series of actions. But it was all a perverted orgy, done in a dream-like, unreal mental state.

She couldn't help thinking of Frank. Wanting Frank.

They rested somewhere along the way, then Sam was assaulting her flesh with his hands and lips.

And, strangely enough, she wanted him to totally devour all thought, awareness, to capture her anguished needs and totally rip them out of her in his violent bestial demands.

Emotions ripped at Jean, creating an anxious need to be quickly taken.

Jean found herself choking in response to his caressing mouth, in response to the warm moisture of his rough tongue.

She felt a tremble convulse through her body and then, all at once, she was bathed in the mounting pleasure that burst through her.

* * * * * * *

Jean stirred in the blackness and sat up. Her

mind was foggy and dazed and for a moment she didn't know where she was. Then remembrance returned and she moved from the bed, not looking at the man. She stepped toward the bathroom and moved into the stall shower. The water sprayed over her body, soothing it, taking away the dirt and sweat of passion. Yet, at the same time, it seemed to bring a desire and need to her.

Jean wasn't aware of movement, and she wasn't aware of the man stepping into the bathroom. Only when the shower door opened did she become alive to what was happening.

Sam was completely naked; he stepped under the shower with her, closing the door behind him.

"What—"

"I thought it would be nice!" he told her, cupping a hand to one of her breasts. His eyes examined her, and then his other hand slid along her stomach. "You're a real live one!" he rasped in a husky voice. "Never had one like you before."

She didn't know if what he said was meant to be nice or not, but decided not to think about it.

Sam grabbed hold of her, and she felt the shower wall against her back. Their bodies squirmed and convulsed and then suddenly he had thrust against her and a moan broke from her lips.

There wasn't any stopping after that; no thought of stopping. Only that dim awareness that this was wrong, but not caring about it, not wanting to care about it. And then, afterwards, they held each other, and she felt the shame and the disgust and horror return. This was cheap and crude. A year before— maybe even a month before—she would have never thought it possible for her to do such a thing. The

175

man was a beast; an animal. A savage. And, per-haps, in some ways, what she needed at that mo-ment in her life. Something that rammed the truth down her mental throat; life offered very little to her.

There were simply very few choices. And none of them seemed desirable. But for the moment this was her reality.

Nothing was said as they stepped from the shower and dried each other. They moved to the bed and Jean knew, with a sickening feeling, what was going to happen. There wasn't any stopping it now; there wasn't any real reason to stop it. And suddenly she knew why it was possible to let this strange man have her. She didn't have anything worth living for—nothing to be moral for, because there wasn't any reason in her life for resisting or restraining de-sire.

What difference did it make? An animal like this man—or a woman like Debra. Both were frowned upon by society as degrading and disgusting.

Joy momentarily overwhelmed Jean as they lay on the bed and the man once more began the acts of passion. It took a long, long time, and when it was over she lay there exhausted. When sleep came she was contented, no fear of dreams tormented her. It had been weeks since the last dream.

But tonight the dreams returned.

The darkness of the room had lightly slipped away and she wasn't really aware when the dream took over from reality. The room was suddenly flooded with light and Frank and Joe and Sam and Debra were standing there, all naked.

Jean tried to move, but couldn't. It was then that

176

she realized somebody had strapped her hands and legs down. She couldn't move, more than an inch. All she could do was lie there watching what took place.

Debra lay on the floor and invited each man to her. And each, in turn took her offering. Jean couldn't see what was happening and everything blurred, but she knew what was happening and a choking sensation sobbed through her throat. Then sudden darkness closed in around her and continued for a long time. When it was that the searching mouth sought her breasts and lips cupped over an erect nipple, Jean didn't know. But she did know it was Debra.

"Please, please, leave me alone!" she cried. "Leave me alone!"

Angrily, she slapped aside the kissing lips and all at once she was in the world of breasts and the ugly little insect men, all of them crawling over her, like tiny black ants.

Jean cried out, terrified.

Quiet surrounded her. Still silence.

"Oh, Frank! I love you. I want you so very much. Don't ask me why, but I want you. I want to marry you and have children. I want a normal home—please take me back—please take me back!" Her voice sobbed in the darkness and then she heard a man's voice at her side.

"Yes—I love you, too. I love you—but you're a Lesbian, and I could never forget that. I would never forget it—and that would ruin all our happiness. You know that!"

"Oh, can't we try? At least, try it out. Attempt to make a go at it. I'll live with you—I don't care—I

*just want a chance! I don't want you to be my
'Megi!' I don't want to grow old, never knowing
what it might have been like with you. Can't we
have that chance? Can't we give it a try and find out
how it might have worked out? Give me that much. I
made a mistake—with Debra Channings—but I
didn't want it—it just happened. Can't you understand that? Can't you understand that I'm normal
and like it only with men?"*

"You're a Lesbian. A Lesbian. A Lesbian. A
Lesbian!"

A Lesbian.

Lesbian.

The word formed itself before Jean's eyes.

L-E-S-B-I-A-N!

"No!" *she screamed.*

Jean was suddenly awake, clutching at her face.

"No! No, I'm not!"

For a moment she was dazed and unsure of herself and then movement on the bed reminded her of
Sam.

"Take me home" she whispered. "Take me
home."

"You kidding? It's the middle of the night!"

The anger and nastiness in his voice startled
Jean.

"I'm going home—if you take me or not!"

The man just turned over, ignoring her.

After a moment she moved from the bed,
dressed in the darkness and stepped out of the motel
room. An hour later she was in her apartment.

That night she didn't sleep, and in the morning
she took a long walk, trying to find some solution to
her loneliness and frustration. But no answer came.

Chapter Eleven

Several days passed by, and Jean's mind continued to have the horror-dreams, each night worse than the night before, until her nerves were raw from lack of real rest. She had gotten into a habit of having several strong drinks before going to bed. She would come home after work, take off her clothing and sit and watch television on the set she had bought a couple of weeks before. What little she ate in the evening was coupled with a martini or whiskey on-the-rocks. She managed a state of light drunkenness until bedtime and then several drinks would pass her to unconsciousness. That was the only way she could face sleep and the dreams, which came with it.

Most of the times, Debra was in them; all the time, Frank. And every time she would awaken in a bath of cold sweat.

Then one evening her phone rang. For a moment she almost didn't answer it; then she stepped over to the phone stand and picked up the receiver.

"Yes?"

"Jean?"

She recognized the voice with a start of surprise. It was Mary.

"What do *you* want?" Bitterness was ugly in her

voice.

"Please, Jean, give me a chance." There was silence and then Mary said in a high-pitched nervous voice, "I know what I did was wrong—but can you forgive me? It was horrible—and I know how wrong I was."

There was heavy silence, and for a long time Jean didn't know quite what to say. Hatred at what her sister had caused to happen—or allowed to happen, which was the same thing, made Jean want to hang up. But the loneliness that had been pushing at her emotions was something else. It was this last that held her. *She needed someone! Anybody!*

Mary finally continued: "Jean—I found the letter and was a...no, I wasn't really shocked—you had told me something about it—but I guess I wanted to strike out at something...somebody! I was so confused; you don't know! And...well, everything has worked out between Joe and me, now—but *then,* I didn't—please try to forgive me. It's not right that sisters should be—be this way. I know what you must think about me. I know you're not...not one of those..."

"Say it! Does the word seem dirty or—"

"Okay. *Lesbian.* I know you aren't. I also know it's possible for a woman to get all confused and do things which...well, she's sorry about. Can't you understand what I'm trying to say?" The voice in the receiver choked, and Jean realized that Mary was crying; and suddenly she softened and knew there wasn't anything to really forgive. Merely to forget.

"Forget it, Mary," she said in a shaking voice.

There was a long awkward silence and then

Mary said, "Can't we get together? And...well, be like we used to be?"

For a bitter moment she fought the desire to simply hang up, hurt Mary back as much as possible. Only that would have been totally counterproductive. Mary had her husband. Jean had nothing but herself, and it was terribly lonely being so isolated in the world. Taking a deep breath, she said: "Why not? That's all gone and forgotten."

"Where're you living?" Mary asked. "The operator wouldn't give me the address."

Jean told her and then said, "I'm glad you called, Mary. You don't know how much it means to me...it's been so lonely—so terribly lonely!"

Emotion choked through her, knifing at her lungs and throat, blinding her eyes.

"Why don't you come home—stay with us?"

After a moment Jean gained control of herself and said, "No—I'm beginning to build a life here...I have to be on my own." For a moment she almost asked if Mary had heard from Frank, then quickly dropped the idea. That would have been a counterproductive question.

"Could I come over, this evening?" Mary inquired. "Me and Joe. We want to make things up to you—any way we can. Believe me."

Jean considered and then nodded to herself. The only emptiness inside her was that Frank couldn't be there, too. But that was a dead, lost issue.

"Yes, that would be nice. When can I expect you?"

"In about an hour?"

They said good-bye and Jean hung the receiver on the hook. She stood there for a long time, emotion waving happily through her. Then suddenly it all slipped away and seemed all so empty. Who could really help her? *What* could really help her? She sighed and went into her bedroom and started getting dressed.

It was a little short of an hour when the bell rang. Jean stepped eagerly forward and opened the front door. Then, startled, she stepped back. Her nerves tightened, confusion flushed her face and suddenly her hands were shaking.

Frank Martin was standing there.

"What the hell are you doing here?" Jean demanded in a weak voice.

"I *had* to see you—Mary arranged things so that—"

Sudden nausea raced up through Jean. Fear and frustration made her weak.

"Get out!" she screamed, not really understanding why she was screaming.

"Please give me a chance." Frank stepped boldly forward and slammed the door behind him. "I have to talk to you!"

"Leave me alone!" Jean didn't know why she suddenly felt so dizzy, but the sight of Frank, standing there, had left her drained. Instinct and desire cried for her to reach out to the man and let him fold her into his strong arms. Pride and anger and pain held her back.

"I know how silly this all must seem to you," Frank began softly. "I only knew you a little while—we hardly know each other. But—damned if I can get you out of my mind."

"What's the use?" Jean asked, tightly, control slowly filtering through the nerves and muscles of her body.

"Plenty of use. All I know is that I want to be with you, Jean. I want to find out what there really is between us...if it's real or just a momentary thing. I can't stand this 'hanging'.... It broke off at the peak!" His face was heavily drawn; his eyes had a determined and fixed look about them. "Jean—I've never reacted to a woman like I reacted to you. Maybe because the buildup that Joe and Mary gave me turned out to be nothing to the reality of you. I was kinda interested, intrigued, before even meeting you. Maybe that's why it hit me so hard. I don't know, and I don't want to think about it any more—or question it! The fact is that I have to know if you can just give me another chance. Can't we try? That's all I wanted to tell you."

"I thought you could always 'smell' a Lesbian...don't you know that's what I am?"

Frank laughed, nervously. "I don't believe it. I've had a lot of time to think that one over. Forget the past. I've never known a woman like you—you're as passionate as any woman I've ever known—and more so...And it *isn't* possible to fool a man!" She started to say something, but Frank waved her aside with his hand. "I know I said it was possible. And maybe it is—for some women—a certain type but you aren't that kind of woman. Not that kind of person. That much I do know without any doubt."

"How do you know?" she demanded bitterly, wishing he would leave. It was too much of a temptation. She was too desperate; too needy.

"What does anybody really know? Nothing! We just struggle and try to make the best out of our lives. That's all anybody knows about himself. That's all we *can* know. Make the best of things. The past can be forgotten. You don't have to live in the past! You don't have to be damned by it. Forget it. Live for today. Let tomorrow take care of itself— develop in its own way, without any resistance. Without fighting the obvious.

"I don't know what tomorrow will bring. But I *do* know that it'll be a living hell if you don't promise to let me take you out to dinner!"

Jean stared at Frank for a long time and then silently walked to the door and opened it. "You had better leave. It'd never work out."

Frank turned and looked helplessly at her. "Why won't you give it a try?"

She didn't say anything.

Frank shrugged and moved to the door. "All I can say is that if you ever change your mind…"

Without warning, he reached for her and pulled her into his arms.

For a moment she felt herself melting, giving in, and then she stiffened and forcefully pushed him away. Without another word he turned and walked out of the apartment and down the hall. She watched him and then after a moment closed the door.

Anger and tears were mixed as Jean leaned back against the wall, her hands clutched to her face. The world spun and the horrid images of the world of breasts with those hateful little insect men formed, then was followed by the image of Debra reaching up for her, begging to be taken back into her life. She pushed those thoughts away, and found herself remembering the cheap motel room she had shared with the strange man named Sam. It all came tumbling down like a vortex into her mind.

Emotion choked Jean's lungs and throat and she was suddenly running down the hall, down the steps and out onto the street.

She spotted Frank getting into his car on the opposite side of the street.

Jean shouted, without knowing what it was she said. She ran frantically toward him, sobs bursting from her throat.

Frank paused and turned.

"Frank, oh, Frank!" Jean cried, rushing into his arms. "Forgive me. Forgive me."

For a few moments he tenderly held her and then slowly and gently pushed her away.

"Come on—" he said in a soft voice, leading her back toward the apartment.

When they had closed the door behind them, Frank lifted her into his arms and carried her into the bedroom.

During the next few hours he made love with a gentleness and with an urgency that revealed the deep emotional feelings within him. Over and over he breathed in her ear his words and sighs of love until a joy and a completeness had filled Jean's very soul with pure happiness. For now she felt no doubt about being normal; a normal woman with normal female passions, and possessed by a normal love for a man.

For the first time in her life she felt that everything was perfect, the way it should be. And she knew that for the time being, at least—and that was all she could hope or wish for—she was desperately in love with Frank and that he would be with her, loving her, until that time when they either blended their souls in marriage, like their bodies had been blended this evening, or they would gently drift apart like two ships passing in the lonely sea at night. But the most important thing was that they were together, now, and that tomorrow could bring what it might.

She wasn't running away, this time. Never again.

That night her dreams were quiet and happy and lovely, as she was sure they would be for the rest of her life, now that the long search was over.

When she awoke the next morning, with her lover at her side, she knew that this was merely the first of many mornings beside Frank. His tender words, which rushed eagerly from his lips as he pulled her to him, gave truth to her inner conviction that their tomorrows would be spent together.

The past had been forgotten, and the future would hold no "Megi" for either of them.

About the Author

Charles Nuetzel was born in San Francisco in 1934, and writes:

"As long as I can remember I wanted to be a writer. It was a dream I never thought would materialize. But with the help of Forrest J Ackerman, who became my agent, I managed to finally make it into print.

"I was lucky enough not only in selling my work to publishers but also ending up packaging books for some of them, and finally becoming a 'publisher' much like those who had bought my first novels. From there it as a simple leap to editing not only a science-fiction anthology, but also a line of SF books for Powell Sci-Fi back in the 1960s. Throughout these active professional years I had the chance to design some covers and do graphic cover layouts for pocket books & magazines."

Much of his work in covers and graphics are a result of having had a father who was a professional commercial artist, and who did a number of covers for sci-fi magazines in the 1950s and later for pocket books—even for some of Mr. Nuetzel's books.

In retirement he has become involved in swing dancing, a long time lover of Big Band jazz. But more interestingly world travels have taken him (and his wife Brigitte) across the world, to Hawaii, Caribbean, Mexico, Kenya, Egypt, Peru, having a lifelong interest in ancient civilizations. His website is full of thousands of pictures taken during these trips.